BLAUSTEIN'S KISS

Blaustein's Kiss

Stories by Judith Felsenfeld

Epigraph Publishing Service
Rhinebeck, NY

LIFE LIST Whiskey Island Magazine   Winter 1996
LOVESICKNESS Chicago Review   Volume 44, No. 4   Winter 2002/2003   originally published as HER LOVER
ROSIE Southwest Review   Volume 85, Number 4   2005
SHAYNA KUPP Southwest Review   Volume 87, Number 4   2005
SOUPGREENS Wisconsin Review   Volume 34, Issue 1   Fall 1999
THE GIFT Blue Mesa Review   Issue Seventeen   2003
THE LOVER Potpourri Magazine   Volume 11, No. 1   1999

Book design by Danielle Ferrara

Library of Congress Control Number: 2013955801
ISBN: 978-1-936940-64-6

Epigraph Books
22 East Market Street, Suite 304
Rhinebeck, NY 12572

Printed in the United States of America

to FREDRICA JARCHO
who got me onto the track
and HELEN HYMAN
who kept me there.

CONTENTS

ACKNOWLEDGMENTS

I am deeply grateful to Sierra Frost and Tim and Susan Millas for their tremendous faith, help and support.

I thank my writing buddies: Connie Biewald, Jenny Burman, Lisa Fugard, Gwynne Guzzeau, Carole Kaufman, Judi Kolenda, Sue Mellins, Candace Perry, Mary Otis, Eileen O'Toole, Marjorie Saunders and Anne Walsh for their friendship, insightful critiques and encouragement over the long haul.

At the Fine Arts Work Center in Provincetown, Massachusetts, I was taught by the best: Robin Becker, Michael Cunningham, Peter Ho Davies, Allan Gurganus, Pam Houston, Dan Mueller and Grace Paley.

Lenore Maroney and Dottie Distel provide a tranquil and beautiful place to work, kindness and companionship–their own and that of many dogs, horses, sheep, and eagles.

And finally I thank my husband, Carl, and Peter and Vida.

SHAYNA KUPP

THE SHRILL OF THE phone jolts her awake and Laura grabs for it too eagerly, collapsing the delicate balance of books and journals stacked on the bedside table.

"Jessie sweetheart, how are you? Hang on a minute. I knocked some stuff down when I grabbed the phone." Briefly she half-hangs from the bed, eyeing the damage. Straightens up. "I'm back."

"When'd you get in?"

"About half an hour ago. The sunlight was so glorious in the bedroom I lay right down on the bed. Didn't even take off my grown-up clothes."

"I guess we take it for granted out here. The sun, I mean. How was the play last night?"

"You know, I love opening nights. You can smell the optimism."

"Not much of a play?"

"You got it. How's the baby?"

"Fine, fine. Mom, listen. We're planning a Seder, a communal Seder, and we want you to come out for it. It will be pot-luck and vegan and a totally different species from Cousin Fran's, I know, but Paco and I really hope you'll—"

There is no possibility, of course. Laura waits for Jessie to wind down, then: "Sweetheart, potluck is a brilliant idea and of course I'd love to be with you and Paco and the baby. But you know. Every year of my life I've been at this Seder. My grandmother and then Aunt Ida and now Cousin Fran."

"Just think about it. Please."

Laura allows a niggling thought to surface. "Listen, I know how busy you guys are, but any chance you could come East instead? Paco has never been to our Seder and now with the baby…" Her brain clicks into high gear. "Frannie will have room for you, without a doubt. I bet Rachel's highchair is still in their basement. It would make the Seder perfect. No pressure. Just think about it. The plane tickets are on me. I mean, even Legal Aid lackeys deserve a little time off." She shifts the receiver to her other ear. Rests on an elbow. "Funny. When the phone rang I was sure it was Fran. She still calls to invite us, every year. Even though everyone takes it for granted."

"I bet she's exhausted. I mean, that wedding."

"You're right." Laura nods. "She probably is still recovering from the wedding. Mother of the bride, after all. Did I tell you how beautiful she looked?"

"Brides always do. It's a law."

"No, not Rachel. I meant Frannie."

She repulses any self-pity at being denied the absurd, frenzied bliss of preparing a proper wedding for her daughter. So many decisions: the invitations, the gown, the flowers, the music, on and on. Laura would have adored them all. Paco and

Jessie were married at low tide on the beach at Bolinas. During the vows the best man was stung by a jellyfish. Afterward, in the damp motel room she and Sam picked seaweed from between their toes. Instead she remarks, "It snowed the first year Frannie took over from Aunt Ida. Snow in April. It was so peculiar to look out the window at snow falling on the lilacs. Eighteen years ago."

"Mom—"

"You were sitting right between Daddy and me. You were still calling it filtered fish. I know it's old news, dear, but it's my old news and I cherish it. Listen. Get back to me soon. Kiss Paco and the baby." She presses a tiny pucker sound into the receiver, pauses for Jessie's, and hangs up.

Jessie's kisses, she thinks. "Give Mommy a kiss, sweetheart." The tiny lips pushing into her cheek, arms flung over her neck. Oh God. Her eyes fill. She and Sam were never as alive together as then, in Jessie's baby years. Often on the street she catches herself staring at the clusters of young mothers behind their strollers. If her gaze is overlong, her desire too naked, one or another of them will pointedly stare back.

Outside the broad windows the sun's reflection glistens on the river. God knows she'd been ready for this retirement. Three decades. Thirty years of deciding which artists to support and which not to. Those are the ones that hang over her four years down the line. And there was never the money for adequate support staff. Running into the office on weekend mornings to catch up on the filing, a bagel crammed in her fist.

On the other hand, there were the powerful daily friendships. She misses them a lot. And the occasional glamour. Black-tie openings. Really grown-up clothes. Sam was a knockout in his tux.

But for his fucking heart attack it would all have been different. Five months before her retirement date. Her successor chosen. Damn, the sun's glare is hitting exactly at her line of vision. She twists onto her side—ah, that's better.

Laura prunes her lips downward. She must stop this self-indulgence. Doctor Gerchell was clear on that point. She runs the fingers of both hands through her hair. She adores the largeness of the gesture. Often she holds on and tugs at the roots until her scalp throbs.

Maybe the invitation is waiting in her mailbox at this moment. She'll run down and check. After that the revisions on the Times piece. No, first her cello. But for no more than half an hour. Even then she'll pay a price in the morning, her bowing arm swollen to twice its size.

The elevator crawls downward. The numbers on the panel flash in succession, nine eight seven—She stares beyond them. There was something in Jessie's tone. Tense or—angry is too strong a word—which leads Laura to doubt that they will come. Some other time then. Little Tito will be the fifth generation at that Seder. And it is gratifying that Jessie wants to make one herself. Vegan? Why not? The only problem that comes to mind is the lamb shank.

"Shit. Shit. Shit. Shit." Jessie replaces the receiver and presses her head hard into the punishing wood backpiece of the rocker. Then, as Paco watches she inhales, willing herself to calmness, one hand spread on the infant curved in the patch of warm skin between her newly lavish breasts. The baby stirs, stretches. Jessie tips forward. Directs the tiny lips around her nipple.

"Well, I tried," she calls over her nursing shoulder. "I gave it my best shot, didn't I?"

Meticulously Paco wipes his fingers on a rag—he has been doing quick charcoal sketches of the rocker, Jessie's head over the baby's, curves, all curves. Each time he watches his son suck he feels as if he might split wide open and a stream of love, thick as honey, come pouring out of him. "Si, cara, the best shot. Your Mama will not come around easily. She knows her mind. Like her daughter."

His sensible Jess swims close to the surface these days. Paco does what he can to protect her. Other phone calls have been put off but not this one. He moves up behind her. Hands easy on her shoulders, he nuzzles her dark hair, slides his lips downward to her neck, the tender tip of her clavicle, where the shirt collar gaps out.

"Hey, that tickles," she squirms, her arm shielding the baby.

Deliberately, on his knees now, Paco works his lips down around Jessie's sleeve and onto the back of the infant's fuzzy skull. For a moment the lips part from the nipple. Paco aches to continue the kisses straight down Jessie's front, to the point where the shirt hem flows onto her bare legs and from there, quien sabe? He forces his mind to the problem at hand. "So. What's next? You must call Cousin Fran, no? To figure out another plan."

"What other plan? The Singles Seder at the Y?" Jessie hands up the baby. Begins buttoning her shirt.

"Cara, how can it be that Cousin Fran cannot find one place, one small place for your Mama who takes up barely any space at all? I find this difficult to understand."

"Oh God," Jessie groans, her mother's mouth wide in her face. "It's not about space, it's about other things. I should have smelled it coming." She tips back in the rocking chair. Releases forward. "Momma's always been special in the family. It was no secret her grandparents favored her. The first-born and all that. Of course she delivered the eulogy at Great-Grandma's funeral. It probably never occurred to her to discuss it with anyone. I hadn't realized how much the other cousins resented her. And she certainly has never admitted it to herself." Abruptly the rocking stops. "Families!"

Dios, Paco would die for a cigarette. For Jessie and the baby he has given up smoking but sometimes, like right now, it is hard. He plucks a sucking candy wrapped in cellophane from the pile on the counter top.

"I mean, the wedding. Sticking Mom at that awful table with Irwin's business partners. The whole family is seated together right up near the dais and Mom is stuck in back with people she's never met before. And Mom, the Mistress of Denial: 'Frannie needed me to make them feel special.' And now this."

The discomfort in Fran's voice on the phone had been palpable. "Before the cousins moved it was a different story. But Laura is the only one left of that generation, not counting Irwin and me, and I barely sit down. You know the kids. Wrapped up in their lives. Nannies. Bonuses. I'm not saying she shouldn't come but in my opinion it's not a comfortable situation for her." Here something snide, almost, had crept into Fran's tone. "Maybe your mother needs to face reality. She's no longer the shayna kupp of the family. She's just like the rest of us, another vestigial cousin."

Jessie's stomach roiled for the rest of the day. "How dare she disinvite Momma? And what's all this shayna kupp shit?"

Now her voice rises. "That's when I phoned Rachel to see what was going on. Slights, decades of slights, like tiny splinters. The eulogy. A feather quilt. Great-grandma's engagement bracelet—some crummy strand of seed pearls that Mom probably doesn't know a thing about." Jessie's face tightens with the pain of it. "And Momma babbling on about us coming East for the Seder." She tugs at the roots of her thick hair.

Again that odd gesture, thinks Paco. A reaction to stress, perhaps. This whole business could never happen in Argentina. Especially in his family, half Italian. Nunca. His thought is preempted: Phew. The diaper needs to be changed, pronto. Can it be that all the vegetables intensify the smell? But this is not the moment to suggest it.

Sunlight streams onto Tito, his head resting in the brilliant tail feathers of a parrot embroidered onto a baby blanket. He scrunches his tiny eyes tight, wriggles his head from the glare. Head cupped in one hand, Paco slides him gently out of the sun's reach, turns to the job at hand.

"So the Seder. What shall we do about the Seder, cara, if your Mama will not come?" He feels awful about the problem with Laura, whose name was familiar even before he and Jessie met. In the arts community, Laura Veit of the Grisham Fund was widely admired for her openness to fresh ideas, her encouragement of risk. At her retirement party he had sat with Jessie at the head table. The praise was effusive.

The Veits had treated Paco always with respect. Neither Laura nor Sam raised one word of objection to the marriage, although surely he is not the husband they visualized for their only daughter. One night early on he had spoken these thoughts to Jessie, moonlight pouring onto their nakedness.

"Not so," she had said. "They're not like that. They'll see that we're good together, that I'm happy, and it will be fine."

Now Jessie looks up. "Dumb deadline," she grumbles. "Could you hand me my bag? The Seder business'll have to wait. I can't figure out how to handle the lamb shank anyway."

* * *

Already Laura's forearm is starting to swell. She must remember to take a Mediprine before turning in. She slaps the densely marked pages onto the coffee table. Damn. Why can't her pea-brain remember that the elation at being asked would last at most an hour, and the responsibility lie over her like a hairshirt for weeks afterward. Lavishly she yawns, feeling the wideness travel up through her spine and out her fingertips, then bending, clicks the living room lamps, slips the front door latch and steps out into the silent vestibule.

The guys next door, who taught her to flip the circuit breaker after Sam died, have retired for the night. A thread of music winds from a deep interior room. She has come out at two in the morning and heard it. Once at four. That was in the wipeout months just after Sam's death. Sometimes then she leaned her cheek hard into the door, as if the wood grain itself held healing powers. Now she draws back inside, double-locks the door, shuffles in her slippers down the hall to the dark bedroom where she flicks on both bedside lamps, hers and Sam's.

At the dressing-table Laura lifts a pinky-weight of the imported lifting-moisturizing cream from its gorgeous jar. $300 an ounce. If she were ever moved to prayer, which is unlikely, she thinks with amusement, it would be that no one ever finds out what she spends on creams and lotions. Her creamed finger trails upward over her cheeks toward her hairline. She remembers once, early on, waking to Sam's fingertips grazing her cheek. Can it be that Fran is not making the Seder this year? But surely she would have said something.

Her dresser top is littered with post-its. "Cable appt" "Ballet tx." "Cl Fran a.m." she jots on a blank one and fixes it in a prominent spot. Her eyes drowse over.

"Here she comes, my shayna kupp." Grandma's bosom was covered with flour from the Shabbos cakes. All morning little Laura walked around with a powdery face.

"Who is that ghost in my kitchen? I'm so frightened."

"It's me. Laura. The shayna kupp."

"Oh, thank God. I thought it was a dybbuk. A ghost."

The first grandchild. The only one, for a long time. Ten years. Until "say hello to your new cousin, Frannie." A tiny baby with an ugly face, definitely not a shayna kupp. And soon after, "your new cousin, Shira." Also ugly. And three more after that. But always Laura's was the most shayna kupp. All her growing up life she knew that, absolutely. Then Jessie arrived. The first great-grandchild. Such a commotion. And if Fran and the cousins seemed terse on occasion, resentful even, it would pass. They were family.

How Grandma would have adored Tito. A true shayn kupp, with Paco's mild temperament. Paco. There was a shock, though she had felt immediately, in her gut, what Jessie found so appealing. But how would he ever support them?

"You're dating yourself, my love." Sam had sounded extremely cheerful. "Things have changed. Jessie will support them both."

On her Legal Aid salary? But they had gotten past it. Was there another option?

"A painter?" Frannie had remarked over the phone. "How interesting. Argentine?" The news had leaked like a stain through the family.

The river is a sheet of glass this evening, Orion strung overhead. If Sam were alive they might be tracing the constellations from a freighter in the Aleutians or a tent in the Mara. If Sam were still alive everything, every single thing, would be different. But he had gone and fucked up the plan. Not even a warning. None of the risk factors except a slight hypertension, well under control.

Ideopathic, the cardiologist told her. Fucking ideopathic.

"Ideopathic?" said Jessie. "What does that mean?" It means your father's dead a week before his seventieth birthday, and your mother's dead too, only she hasn't figured it out so she's still walking around. That's what it means, dear.

A wildness grabs at Laura, she swings from the bed, wriggles out of her nightgown, flings the closet door wide to the mirror inside. The moonlight slants onto her in a crazy geometry. She remembers her shock when the first gray appeared in her pubic hairs, and the first thinning. After Sam's death she'd stopped noticing. Now, with effort, she forces her gaze downward. Her bush is nearly gone. Lone gray hairs wisp haphazardly over her naked pubis. Obscene. A swift sudden nausea rises in her throat. She cannot remember ever having seen the genitals of an aging woman before.

That time in the emergency room, the only time she saw her mother completely naked, she was clamped to the terror in her mother's eyes. She could not have looked anywhere but into those eyes. Never? Not in a painting or a photograph? No. Not even in the changing room at the gym. Is there some special place where the old women shower? A shame room?

It takes a moment for the ringing to break through the din in her brain. Laura muddles for the phone, reflexively clutching her breasts. "Yes. Hello."

"Mom, it's me."

"Jessie, what's up? How's the baby?"

"Fine. I just felt like saying hello." Jessie's voice pours through the phone line. "Bad moment? You sound weird."

"Just surprised." With her free hand she tugs at the top sheet.

"You weren't asleep?"

"No. Washing up. You know, routine maintenance."

"Yeah, I know. Wrist cream, pinky cream—"

This makes Laura laugh. "Dear God, am I so transparent?"

"About some things."

"Sweetheart, you must have felt the vibes. I was feeling a little raw just now."

"I'm a pro at vibe reading. Any more thoughts about coming out for the Seder?"

"No chance, dear. I'm sorry. Did you talk to Paco?"

"He really really hopes you'll change your mind. Don't close your mind, please. Think about it. He's already teaching Tito the Four Questions."

"Some wunderkindt. Surpassing even his grandmother. And you've heard about me."

Jessie, dryly: "More than once."

"Sweetheart, why such a big deal? If not this year, then next. Which reminds me, I still haven't heard from Fran. I guess I'll make the chorosis again. I assume she's counting on it."

Jessie's reply is unintelligible.

"Come again?"

"Love you, Mom."

"What was that, about Fran?"

"What? No. Nothing."

"Oh. Love you too, dear. 'Night."

Laura tunnels her face into the pillow, grunts, slips to a place beyond dreaming.

* * *

In the thin morning light Laura places her coffee mug onto the bedside table and, favoring the bad arm, climbs back under the sheets. Reaches for a long gulp. Then she places the telephone onto her lap. She'll wait until eight thirty, just in case. Even though Frannie is long awake, she has no doubt. Of course she'll bring the chorosis, she'll say. Unless Fran prefers something else. The coffee slides down soothingly.

Outside, the river is stirring. A commuter ferry slides from its slip, a tug zigzags in the wake of a freighter heading upstream. Where will she be seated this year? Not with the new in-laws, she hopes. Irwin's partners swim into her line of vision, still in their wedding clothes. Stylish women, bulky, solicitous men. What a shame that Paco and Jessie won't be there with the baby. Where would she choose to sit? Her mind prowls the crowded table: the kids at the far end, texting under the tablecloth. There's a familiar face. Frannie's neighbor. Or is it the woman she shared her office with? The fact is, there is no right place for her. How can that be? The words loom large behind her eyelids. There is no right place—She reaches unsteadily for the mug. No, better wait. She breathes deeply. The telephone presses hard onto her knees.

"Careful, careful," she would cry when Sam swung the baby, Jessie, in the air. "She's fragile." As Laura feels at this moment. Fragile. No. She needs critically to find the right words. Bruised. Damaged.

A horn blasts and the commuter ferry pulls from its Jersey slip. Laura sits unmoving, her eyelids tight. She inhales, releases the air in a long stream. A crowd clusters at the bow of the ferry, briefcases dangling. Yes, she must call Frannie. Explain about Paco and Jessie's Seder. Apologize for breaking the tradition. Send her love to everyone. Perhaps next year, she'll say, in an upbeat tone of voice. She'll end on a humorous note: Tell Irwin he must take you away for a serious rest after the Seder. Tell him Cousin Laura said so.

She reaches for the post-it pad. Suddenly there's a lot to do. Dmitri, the super, will water her plants, no problem. She must phone the airline, get the super to bring the big suitcase down from the hall closet, dig out her cotton pantsuits. The weather should be perfect in the Bay Area this time of year.

THE GIFT

THE GIRLS NEVER STOPPED torturing her. Hi Emma, Hi Emma. In the yard, in the coatroom. Forcing the "H" into the air. On the way to school. From school. Hiyemma. If five of them were walking together down the street it came five times. The child didn't have a moment's peace.

I saw her once coming from Gina's, carrying some tomatoes, it looked like, a head of iceberg, her face soft (which was not usual, she was an anxious child), her thoughts floating toward the clouds—a trip to Bear Mountain perhaps, the happy ending to the story she just finished reading—when they spotted her. Hiyemmahiyemma. She turned herself into the smallest possible dot, like the period at the end of a sentence, and scurried into a shadow.

Every Saturday ten a.m., you could set your clock by it, on the way to her piano lesson, they were there. Even with her mother at her side, she who had complained to the principal last year about the lack of music appreciation in the classroom, causing him to bring in a radio and make everyone listen to thirty minutes straight of classical music. Only then the syllables slid out in singsong through pasted-on smiles. Hi Emma hi Mrs. Shein.

Then the game changed. New rules: from now on everybody was Emma. It's clear in my mind's eye: One morning Mona says to Ginger, with one of those eye-smiles, hi Emma, and Ginger says it right back, and by recess everyone in Grade 4A is called Emma.

Most days Emma herself came out late to the yard. She would stand blinking on the pavement, always a piece of hair twisting in her top teeth, and then walk over to the bench at the shady end where Catherine Fedoryko sat, recovering her strength after diptheria. All these years I have never heard an explanation of where that poor child contracted a disease that had already been eradicated. Anyway, Emma would perch on the farthest end, push up her glasses with her nose, and open her book. She was always reading. Always. Walking to and from school. In the mornings before Mrs. Lynch came into the classroom. Once Mona saw her walking down the street reading, and when she bumped into a hydrant she begged its pardon. The other girls nearly died laughing when Mona told them.

When recess is over it starts again. Hiyemma, hiyemma. On line behind Mrs. Lynch, Emma twists her head to Ginger, who is constantly behind her, size place, like a hairshirt, and mutters under her breath to cut it out.

Ginger hisses like the snake she is, "Cut what out?"

Mrs. Lynch doesn't take the trouble to turn her pinhead. "Do I hear talking?"

"Saying my name."

"Your name? No one's saying your name. It's just a name. Emma. It's a free country, right? Anyone can say any name they feel like, right?"

Mrs. Lynch announces that someone in the class is going to stay after three o'clock if she hears one more word. Tight tears are oozing down Emma's cheeks. Her lips are twisted in and she's pressing down hard on them. I personally have seen that look on her face hundreds of times. Somebody whispers out loud, "Crybaby."

II

The gift problem went way back. You had to give the teacher a Christmas present no question, no matter if you were Jewish Christian Hindu. Also it made no difference if she was Jewish Christian Hindu whatever. A handkerchief or a bottle of Shalimar Eau de Cologne. What else could you get for a dollar fifty, which is what most children had to spend? In some families the mother would crochet a doily, but mostly it was the boring handkerchief or the boring cologne, year after year.

That December, S. Klein featured in its window a gorgeous silk scarf with golden threads pulled through, eleven ninety-five. Mona was crazy about it. So of course her friends were, too. They carried on about that scarf non-stop, passing notes back and forth on bits of paper torn from the back pages of their speckled notebooks. But where could any of them lay their hands on eleven ninety-five? Which Lindy reminded the others didn't include tax. Her father was an accountant.

Now here comes a crucial scene. The girls are bunched in a corner of the coatroom on Monday morning discussing their dilemma when Emma walks in to hang up her coat. All at the same instant, like the Rockettes, they drop their arms to their sides and freeze in place. A new torment. The latest addition to the repertoire. Maybe ten days old so Emma is already accustomed to it. In any case, she does not react. She removes a string of hair from between her lips and works it under the sidepiece of her eyeglasses. Shapes her lips. Re-shapes them. Says, "My mother had an idea. For the scarf."

Simultaneously they suck in their cheeks and look to heaven.

"Pray tell," says Mona.

"If everyone put their dollar fifties together there'd be enough money." Emma's face looks like it wishes it had nothing to do with the words coming out of her mouth.

"Cretin," says Ginger.

"Hmmm," says Mona.

Lindy informs the constituency that a dollar fifty times seven equals ten fifty.

Emma, so low you have to lean in to catch it: "I could put in the last dollar fifty if you want."

Ginger slants her face to a dangerously irritated angle.

"It was her mother's idea," Mona reminds them. They nod. This is true.

In the end they hiked it up another nickel to a dollar fifty-five, to cover the tax and also a nonreligious Christmas card, the majority of these children coming from Jewish homes, which they would all sign. Lindy was the money-monitor, hiding it in an envelope in her desk top, the bills all laid out perfectly flat, facing the same way. With the coins tucked in a back corner. Friday after school they would take the bus to S. Klein's to shop. Mona would keep the gift in her bedroom until Monday morning when all together they would present it to Mrs. Lynch. Amen.

And suddenly Emma is one of them. Mona invites her to Hi-Mark's for an egg cream after school. And when Emma can't come because she has to go home to practice, they all walk her to her corner backwards, lurching and giggling and falling into one another and taking up the whole sidewalk. And while they're waiting for the light to change, Emma tells them how much she hates practicing but there is no choice because she has a gift. And unfortunately it looks like her little brother might have the same gift. And that Catherine Fedoryko lives in a cellar on Second Street with no toilet. And her brothers and sisters stink even worse than she does.

So day by day the glorious week passes. The sun shines every single moment and not a cat yowls in fear or anger on the streets. The light from the sun setting on the Hudson meets the light from the East River, casting enchantment in the late afternoons, and breezes blow the fresh smells of the Second Street bakery throughout the neighborhood.

Friday Emma comes into school with her cheeks stained and behind her glasses swollen eyes. Her new friends bustle around her, pressing and patting and passing her Kleenex like a contest: who can show the most sympathy the quickest. Her mother, she of the brilliant chipping-in plan but ambitious for her child beyond reasonableness, will not permit Emma to miss the day's piano practice. Why is it necessary that she travel all the way to Fourteenth Street after school? Her money is handed in. The scarf is already chosen. The other girls will do the shopping. Emma has more important things to do. She must keep priorities in mind.

The girls are extremely sympathetic. They say again and again that Emma need not worry: she has handed in her money, the scarf is already selected, they will sign her name on the card. Ginger promises to teach her how to jump in, during recess.

Monday morning Emma arrives with her face lit up like a menorah on the eighth night. The present stands handsomely wrapped in the center of Mrs. Lynch's desk, with the card in its white envelope pasted on top. A piece of holly is stuck under the ribbon.

There is a stillness in the room. Emma finds the girls huddled near the blackboard.

"Hi," she says with an eye-smile that includes them and the present on the desk.

"Hi," they answer awkwardly.

There is shoving and some jostling. A slip of paper is passed hand to hand into Mona's, who is propelled from the middle into the space between them and Emma. She holds out an envelope halfway.

"Here. The scarf was marked down. To ten dollars. So we didn't need your money. So here."

Emma looks at her as if Mona is talking in tongues. From inside the group someone coughs.

"We didn't sign your name on the card. I mean, we didn't use your money so—" Mona stops.

One by one the candles extinguish on Emma's face. She twists a thread of hair into her mouth, extends a weightless hand for the envelope.

Lindy mutters under her breath, "I said we should've—"

Mona melts backwards into the girls, who are turning into a clump. With no eyes, no mouths, no shape.

You know, to make music is a wonderful thing. Often in my life I've wished I could play an instrument. A flute, perhaps. Anyway, that's the end of the story. I heard that a few of the girls felt ashamed. Which probably made them act even meaner for a while. Some business.

A HAT STORY

ELLIS ISLAND 1916

Hirsch Meyer yawns and scratches his chest through his shirt. The room is filthy. God knows what diseases you could catch just sitting here. Personally he is having big doubts about the whole business. They have been waiting on this hard bench for how many hours now? At least three. And the noise! Crying, arguing, most often in a harsh language neither Yiddish nor English, irritating to the ear. Who knows what they are saying? Who knows when finally Mirka and the little girl will come through the door? He was a fool to have agreed to this.

How many have come through already? He stopped counting at sixty. The air stinks: garlic, tobacco, piss. Why doesn't someone open another window? He might try to nap if Leib would sit still, for God's sake. The man is a nervous wreck. Up, down, pacing, twitching, lighting a cigarette, stomping it out after three short puffs, reaching into his pocket for another.

Ah, the door is opening. Every face in the room swings to it. Maybe this time. The Immigration Officer in his gray uniform steps through, followed by a muscular fellow clutching a small sack with all his wordly belongings, who blinks into the smoke-filled air. Ponasero, the Immigration official booms. And again, Ponasero.

Dario, mio caro fratello. A young woman clambers over the back benches to the middle aisle. Finalmente.

Hirsch Meyer relaxes his considerable bulk downward into his midsection. Tugs from his pocket a hunk of prune danish wrapped in waxed paper, shoves it into his mouth, glances sidelong at the poor nebbish twitching next to him on the bench. That absurd homburg. Who does he think he is, President Wilson? Personally he had big doubts about this Leib from the beginning.

* * *

The news had come in a letter from Rifka, Hirsch Meyer's eldest sister. His wife, Gussie, crept down the back stairs to the bakery to hand it to him, despite the pain in her bad leg. After all, how often did a letter come from the old country? These days, seldom.

His baby sister, Mirka, was engaged to marry Leib, the brother of their sister Chanah's husband. Period. That was the sum total of the information. Imagine sending a letter with so little information. Hardly worth the postage.

Then the usual paragraphs of complaints: the bins in the market were nearly empty—the Army took what they needed first and 1912 had been a poor summer for the crops in any case; a pogrom in the next town; talk about war. So what else was new? Rifka: stingy with everything, food, smiles, words.

Hirsch Meyer had wondered which Leib this was, anyway.
He could remember three in the village of perhaps an appropriate
age. Which one had a brother? How could he be expected to
remember any of this? It was ancient history. He was raging now,
his fists clenched, his face dangerously red. Gussie sighed. Such
a temper. Thank goodness the bakery was empty. She hobbled
quickly up the back stairs.

Behind the counter Hirsch Meyer railed on under his
breath. So who exactly was this Leib? And how would he support
little Mirka? His favorite. A delicate child, soft-spoken, discreet,
pacifying. In Hirsch Meyer's mind she was still twelve years old
and he was saying goodbye to her with his eyes across the supper
table, although she had no way of knowing that. In the morning
he was off to America. Before the family awoke. Except his
father, davenning the morning prayers, who would not even look
up. Would he ever see her again? Probably not. Good luck then,
Mirkale. His chest filled with a strange new weight: melancholy.

A year passed, and another few months. Another letter.
From Mirka this time. She ran quickly through a few catching-
up sentences: the second eldest brother had moved with his wife
to Warsaw; several babies had been born—to this sister, that
sister-in-law. The names were barely familiar. And in the second
paragraph: times were bad. The new year did not look promising.
Now she, Mirka, was pregnant and Leib was coming to America.
Possibly, could Leib board with Gussie and him? It would so
greatly relieve her mind. Hirsch Meyer would see immediately
that Leib was industrious. He would work very hard and save up
to send for Mirka and the baby.

Mirka was right. Leib was a worker. Hirsch Meyer found
him a job sewing coat linings and Leib himself found a second
job at night, sweeping out the feathers in a poultry market. He

paid Hirsch Meyer and Gussie the going rate for the half a room he shared with the other boarder and the bathroom down the hall. Every evening he ate his dinner and scurried to his room.

Letters hurried back and forth between Leib and Mirka, often in Mirka's a personal message to her brother, designed to disarm and flatter that ego she knew so well. "How can I ever thank you for allowing Leib to help in the bakery" and "Leib is thrilled that you trust him to babysit for your little girl." Lately an occasional line to Gussie. "I look forward to meeting you and your Faygele. Leib writes that she is intelligent and also musical. Such a child is a blessing beyond measure."

* * *

Leib's stomach growls. He wasn't expecting such a long wait. His own processing had gone quickly. Outside the door, vendors hawk their wares loudly: apples, oranges, dried fruit. But no, he will not spend an extra penny.

He hopes there is no problem. Poor Mirka must be exhausted. And tending to the child as well.

His little girl. Ranah. Almost three. His responsibility, as is Mirka. And soon, next month probably, his brother and sister-in-law will be here. Also his responsibility. Already they are submitting their passports to the authorities. He knows from the Yiddish paper that the war talk in Europe is more than talk. Every worker at the coat factory is frantic to hurry his loved ones out of harm's way. Mirka. Her soft flesh, her breasts. It's been nearly two years. When he left Mokov, they were sore and distended from the nursing. Now it is his turn to suck at the nipples. Grasp her buttocks with both hands, rub his face back and forth along the folds of her belly. He squeezes his lids tight and moans, then jumps to his feet, plucks the cigarette pack from his pocket, extracts one. In his half-sleep, Hirsch Meyer mutters aloud. Leib examines the room. Six seven eight groups left. This morning the benches were completely filled. Is there a bathroom? He will not ask Hirsch Meyer, not unless the situation becomes desperate.

Not a bad man precisely, but not an easy one, quick to criticize, to lay blame. Not an easy man to live with. Ask Gussie. His co-workers at the linings factory wait every morning for Leib's reports of the previous night's theatrics.

Leib tugs his homburg from his head, blots his sweating forehead with the side of his arm. He sees in the Yiddish paper that President Wilson wears a homburg at all ceremonial occasions. Which this is, certainly. The beginning of their new life. Tonight he and Mirka and the little one will sleep for the first time in their own apartment in New York City in America. In a few weeks they must consider bringing in a boarder or two but for now they are alone.

The door opens again. The official steps in. Mokover, he booms. And behind him is Mirka, her face drained of color, the child clinging to her skirt. God in Heaven. The official booms again, Mokover.

Mirka, Mirka. Leib is waving his hands, poking at Hirsch Meyer's arm with his finger. She's here. Sobbing. Running. Mirka.

Papers? requests the official. Leib and Mirka stare at one another across a width of bench.

Papers, papers, the official prods.

Hirsch Meyer chugs up, a broad smile, a grimace almost, covering his face, the precious papers waving in his hand. It's fine, sir. Everything is perfect. Here, the papers.

Mirka steps back, her arms tight around the feather quilt in which are wrapped other treasured objects from home. Ranah, the little girl, pasted to her mother's skirt, stares silently from under a dark head of hair.

Thank you, officer, thank you. Hirsch Meyer returns the papers to his shirt pocket, his face still stretched into the awful smile. He turns now to Mirka and it softens into something genuine. Mirkale. He takes her face in two hands and kisses her cheek. You could use a couple of good meals.

And now the whole warm bundle of Mirka and her quilt and the little girl is moving into Leib's arms. His eyes are streaming. Hers are too.

There is a wail. No no no. The child is shrieking, wriggling with amazing strength.

Sha, what is it, what is happening? Sha. Mirka tries frantically to calm the little girl. Every eye in the room is fixed on them. Sha. It's alright alright here is Papa, Papa, yes it's alright. Shhh. She presses the child into her bosom—the quilt drops—sways from side to side. Shhhh. Here is Papa.

Leib holds out his arms to the child, who cringes backward. A quiet moment. He smiles his most gentle smile, takes a small step, holds out his arms. And again: No no no. The child is beside herself, climbing almost over her mother's shoulder. If she could she would melt into Mirka's skin.

Now here's a mess. Hirsch Meyer turns away in disgust. The man's own child will not come to him. He never imagined such a thing. The man lacks totally a fatherly instinct. Poor Mirka. Whoever heard such a thing? Everyone is staring at them. How much worse can this get?

Mirka is rocking back and forth now, the little girl crushed to her bosom, one hand pressing the curls, the other clutching at the churning legs. It's Papa, Papa, she repeats. Remember, I told you we are coming to Papa in America. Papa who loves you. Calm yourself, Ranale.

Leib's face is ashen. He shrinks into his coat, mortified. His arms hang useless, vestigial.

She's not like this. Mirka feels an urgent need to explain. She's an easy child, friendly, in the village she goes to everyone… It must be the trip. The confusion. Such a long wait in the lines…

Leib bends now to gather up the quilt, the candlesticks, the mortar and pestle, the white lace engagement shawl. The homburg tips from his head onto the floor. He looks up, further chagrined. The child meets his gaze. A hiccup travels visibly through her chest.

Mirka's eyes widen. Leib, it's the hat. The hat. When has she ever seen such a hat? Only on Doctor Sternlieb. He's the only man in the village with such a hat. He never takes it from his head.

The hat? Ach. Leib drop-kicks it with the point of his shoe. It sails over several benches. How could I know? Ranale, it's me, your Papa. Not the bad doctor with the hat. He shakes his bare head. Come, sweetheart. Again he holds out his arms. Solemnly the child shakes her head. No. Not yet, she seems to be saying.

But a few moments later, when they trudge onto the ferry which will carry them to Manhattan, Leib carries in one arm the quilt and in the other the little girl who is resting her full weight on his arm, her head drooping, drooping onto his shoulder.

* * *

So. A touching vignette. I, Ranah's daughter, will hear this story dozens of times. It will bring a chuckle every time, guaranteed. When I am young, Ranah's age, and for a few years afterward, I will find it difficult to picture my mother as a petrified waif so in my mind she will be a different child. Unrelated. Still a good story.

* * *

A RAINY SUNDAY, 1975. MY PARENTS' LIVING ROOM.

Nicky, our three-year-old, is playing cowboy with my father. From the wing chair at the far end of the room, Grandma Mirka follows the action.

"Faster, Grandpa," Nicky hollers as they lumber past, my father on all fours.

My father yells over his shoulder, "If I were you, young fella, I'd get ready for a surprise." Grins up at my mother and me seated side by side on the velvet sectional.

My mother, Ranah, is describing to me, under the clack of her knitting needles, how she had to practically kidnap Grandma Mirka to get her to stay over after Friday's visit to the neurologist. "Three nights, maybe four. Just to keep an eye on her. It's a new medication, after all."

A grainy headshot of Nixon stares up from the newspaper on my lap.

"Will you look at your father? He'll feel it in his knees tonight, guaranteed."

I, softly, "I remember the feeling, bumping along on his back."

My mother, with some asperity, "Which was how many years ago?" She stays her knitting needles. "Nicky," she calls. "Your poor horse needs a drink of water."

"He's not thirsty," Nicky yells back.

Grandma Mirka chortles. "Such a mouth, an answer for everything."

"Alley-oop." With a quick thrust of his backside, my father dumps Nicky onto the carpet. "Time out."

"Owwwww." Nicky flails his limbs comically.

With difficulty my father climbs onto his feet, digs in his pocket for a handkerchief, heads down the hallway toward the bathroom.

Still chuckling, Mirka removes her thick shoes from the hassock. Smooths the bodice of her housedress. Reaches an arm's length to the side for her walker. "I think I'll lie down for a few minutes. Maybe later, Ranale, we'll give the rest of the family a call." She waves aside my outstretched arm.

My mother nods and follows with her eyes—the furrows deepened between them—as Mirka inches down the hall. "I'm worried about your grandmother. She's alone too much. If she should slip..."

"Which reminds me," I cut in. "What about the unveiling? It's nearly six months that Grandpa Leib is gone." The unwelcome awareness flashes through my mind: I haven't really missed him. "Isn't it time to start planning?"

"That's true." My mother sighs. "I've been so wrapped up with Grandma, I've barely given it a thought."

"Daddy, daddy," Nick is yelling and here comes Marc from the kitchen, his cheeks bloated with my mother's signature Rice Krispie-and-marshmallow confection.

"Ranah, these cookies are heaven. I keep saying you should go into the business." He swallows, shifts his attention to Nicky. "Okay, big guy, but now you're the horse."

"Me? That's not how we play."

"Watch out," hoots Marc, "here I come," clasps him around the waist, pins him with a long leg. Nicky slips out from under, giddy with laughter. They lurch into the foyer.

"Lunatics." My mother flaps a hand at them. "They're a joy to watch."

From the foyer come the sounds of joyous battle. My mother takes a sheet of knitting instructions from her bag, peers at it for a long moment. I scan the newspaper headline: Gap In Watergate Tape Still A Mystery. My mother is staring with profound interest at the instruction sheet.

"I never had a good relationship with my father," she says. Outside the window, a gull freezes in midair, a splat of raindrops stops dead in its track down the window glass.

"Mom, what are you saying? Grandpa Leib adored you. He was so proud of your accomplishments: your teaching, your poetry."

"Proud, maybe," says my mother. "But there was always something there…An unease. A tension." She crams the instructions into her knitting bag, pokes the long needle into the bag of wool.

We lived in the same apartment house, for goodness sake, three flights up. How could I have missed it? The newspaper is weightless in my hand.

He was an anxious man, Grandpa Leib. I'll grant that. Always in a rush. The joke in the family is that he walked into a room backwards because he was already planning to leave. Always on the go. Ants in his pants.

But the pressures on him. Three more children in quick succession. Sometimes barely enough money for the essentials, no matter how many hours he worked. And in those bad years Hirsch Meyer and Gussie made themselves scarce, probably fearful they would be asked for help. To me his four children were the glories of his life. Or was I too self-involved to notice?

"What was it? Was he critical? Demanding?"

My mother sighs, "No, no," pushes a few stray ringlets off her forehead with the palm of her hand. "It was deeper than that. You know the story, when Grandma Mirka and I arrived at Ellis Island—"

I lean forward, restless. "Yeah, yeah. Hirsch Meyer and the hat."

"Often I've thought I never got over it. The trauma. The fear."

"Did Grandpa know? Did you talk about it?"

"Don't be silly. Who would talk about such a thing with her father? In those days especially. Maybe today, everybody with their shrinks, their self-awareness…But it was different then. You know that."

I do know. Grandma Mirka travels in her dreams through the long afternoon. Nicky and Marc tumble together. In the kitchen my mother begins trimming the radishes for tonight's salad.

I sit alone on the velvet sectional re-imagining scenes fixed long ago in my mind's eye. The ferry belches fumes into the air. "Hurry, hurry," Hirsch Meyer hollers from the deck as Leib and Mirka hasten towards the gangplank, laden with bundles. Yes, the child, Ranah, is resting in Leib's arms, her head drooping onto his shoulder, but now notice her eyes, pensive, wary, unwilling to trust.

* * *

FEBRUARY 2000

Ranah, my mother, eighty-nine, widowed for many years, succumbs after a long illness. For those closest to her a sense of almost physical loss, of amputation. When we return home from the cemetery a buffet is set out in the dining-el: cold cuts, salads, half-sour pickles, the traditional hard-cooked egg for continuance sliced in thirds for the cholesterol counters. Marc and I watch as Nicky introduces Christina, his fiancee, to the relatives who return with us. An harmonious passage into the family. My mother would approve.

In the living room, family anecdotes are trotted out. Please, not the hat story again. But these stories are of a slightly later vintage, the struggling years, the deprivations, hilarious in retrospect.

My eye catches an elderly woman standing apart. There's a resemblance between us, hard to pinpoint.

"Cousin Faygel, thank you for coming."

"Of course I came." With effort, she turns to face me. "Your mother and I played together as children. Our parents were friends."

"I heard often about Hirsch Meyer and Gussie's kindness to my grandparents."

"Your grandfather Leib actually lived with us but of that I have only a dim memory. I remember especially your grandmother, Tante Mirka. A charming woman. Her life was not easy."

"I'm sure." I shake my head. "Imagine leaving your family knowing you might never see them again." We stand quietly, imagining. I break the mood. "But now, when did you and I last see one another? It must be several years. A wedding or perhaps a bar mitzvah?"

"Most likely it was a wedding, maybe a funeral. I no longer attend bar mitzvahs—too noisy."

Which makes me laugh. "I know what you mean. Come, I'll find you a comfortable chair."

In the living room Marc has opened another bottle of Pinot. More laughter, more stories. This family loves stories.

A few hours later most of the guests are gone. Nick and Christina huddle shoulder to shoulder on the piano bench, their smiles stretched thin. The bottle is empty and my eyes have instructed Marc not to replace it.

I'm exhausted—this day started a long time ago. The cold cuts reek mildly from the dining room. My mother is gone, I'm next in line, is the reality edging into my mind.

On the sofa, an octogenarian uncle is still going strong. "So when she needed the abortion my mother came to help out."

Abortion? Grandma Mirka? What have I missed here?

"Grandma Mirka helped with an abortion? Is that what you're—?"

"And what's so surprising about that?" Cousin Faygel interrupts. "Your grandmother knew a thing or two about abortions. Most women did in those days."

I'm standing up now. Surveying the room preemptively. Who exactly is still here? Nick, Christina, a few cousins slant in from their bridge chairs. That's all right.

"Poor Mirka knew well about abortions," says Cousin Faygel. And she proceeds to tell us about Mirka's pregnancies after the four children. At least two, she remembers. Maybe more. But there was no money for more children. Or enthusiasm, I suspect. And Grandpa Leib was not about to curb his appetites. So there were abortions on the kitchen table. Oh my God.

"Faygel, how do you know this? You were a child."

"Not so young. A teen-ager. Older than Ranah. Your grandmother came to my father, desperate. He found the abortionist, one with a decent reputation, and he paid him, too." Faygel leans in. Gestures to my uncle. "I remember, on those days Leib left early for work. You little ones showed up at our house before breakfast. We fed you, you went to school. Poor Ranah had to stay behind to help."

The scene shifts into focus: the table's everyday oilcloth covered with a layer of towels, Mirka stretched out beneath a worn sheet, her nightgown bunched at the waist. The doctor tips a few sweet-smelling drops of ether from a vial onto a square of gauze. At the head of the table, Ranah grasps her mother's hand hard, turns her face from the doctor's awful business. Afterwards she will ease Mirka's broken weight into the bedroom.

The collective holding of breaths in the living room is palpable. So much for charming stories about hats. Nick rocks abruptly forward on the piano bench; a cousin nods with significance to another. Faygel grunts, releases her weight back into the armchair.

Through the apartment walls a door bangs, an ancient elevator bucks and groans. Outside over the water towers, nimbus clouds drift through a width of sky, the arc of a jet plane breaks the spreading darkness. Any moment now the street lamps will flicker on.

THE LOVER

IN THE MIDDLE OF HER DOWNLIFE plunge into dementia, my mother has taken a lover.

My aunt's voice singes the phone lines. "Who is this George? Phil and I make a special trip to Riverdale to see my only sister, share secrets, discuss family matters, and we spend the whole visit talking politics with some old man."

"I don't know much more than you do, Gert. His name is George Gelman. He's lived at the Home for about three years. He and Mom seem very fond of each other."

"He'll drop her like a hot potato when he finds out she can't remember anything. Then you'll have a real problem on your hands."

My mother and George are inseparable. They walk through the corridors hand in hand and the residents part before them. Her lipstick is always smeared.

* * *

"Shall we invite George to join us?" I ask my mother on the phone. Today is our weekly lunch date.

"Who?" she asks.

"George Gelman, your gentleman friend."

"Oh, you mean my fella. Yes. Good idea."

They are bundled in scarves and overcoats when I arrive.

"I was about to invite you to lunch but it looks as if someone already has." George beams. "Your mother has tendered the invitation. It will be a pleasure." As we walk toward the car, I note that my mother has delicately slowed her step so that George can keep pace. He holds open the door on the driver's side for me, then plods to the side door where my mother waits and tucks her in before seating himself in back. Through the rearview mirror I watch him laboriously angle his body into the car and it occurs to me that one side of him may not work anymore.

"My daughter and I often come here," George remarks as I steer us into a parking space outside the diner. The waitress greets him warmly and leads us past the dessert carousel to the corner booth.

"The regular?" she asks.

"What else?" he confirms.

My mother stares wide-eyed at the menu. Appetizers, Entrees, Cold Sandwiches, Hot Sandwiches, Salad Plates, Soups, From the Griddle, Bagels Plus.

"I'm in the mood for pancakes, Mom. What about you?"

"Good idea."

"Decaf on the side?"

"Fine."

George is twinkling all over. The waitress returns with three orders of pancakes, decaf on the side.

"A remarkable coincidence," George proclaims. "We are all on the same wavelength."

My mother pats his jacket sleeve. He puts an arm around her and squeezes her shoulder. I am about to burst with joy. But in the tender pre-dawn hours I am disquieted. "I feel I should be protecting her in some way," I tell Paul. "What if he forgets to wake up tomorrow morning? Mom would be devastated."

"The world is full of what ifs, love. Relax. Enjoy it. It's quite a coup when you figure the ratio of men to women in that place. Your mother is one of the most attractive women there—definitely a ten on the Riverdale scale."

"But what will happen when he realizes she can barely follow a conversation?"

"He probably knows already. How could he not? Maybe he thinks it's adorable. Maybe his memory problem is so bad he can't remember that she has one."

"Paul, please. This is not a joke."

"Of course it's not a joke. It's a friendship that is currently bringing pleasure to two elderly people. I mean, face it. We aren't exactly discussing a long-term commitment here."

* * *

George had clerked for thirty-eight years in the Municipal Court. Shortly after his wife's death he suffered a stroke and his daughter persuaded him to move into Riverdale Park. It turns out to have been an excellent decision. He is active on the Social Policy Committee and has begun working in ceramics. His daughter, Carol, who teaches at Vassar, drives down on the weekend.

'I'm eager for you and Carol to meet," says George. "It won't surprise me if you two become fast friends."

George's knowledge of my mother's life is spotty at best. I search for openings.

"Paul sends his love, Mom. His book is moving along. The first draft should be done in the next few weeks."

"What is your husband's field?" George asks.

"Sociology, specifically prison reform."

"A critical concern. And have your children followed in their parents' footsteps?"

"No. They're both in the sciences."

The waitress refills my cup.

"There was a store near our apartment in Brooklyn that sold all kinds of exotic coffees."

"We lived in Brooklyn?" my mother asks.

"On Eastern Parkway, Mom. Across from the Museum. You taught fourth grade then, remember? You were Teacher of the Year for three years running. We were so proud."

"We?" asks George.

"My dad and my kid brother and I. He died in a car accident at college. I sometimes think my father never got over it. He died of a heart attack eighteen months later."

The table is still. I am aware of something clenching inside as it always does when my brother comes up.

"My wife also passed away after a heart attack. I thought that I would never be happy again."

That night I get down the old photo album that sat for years on an end table beside the couch in my parents' living room. In an early snapshot—"Coney Island, 1932" is written on the back in my mother's hand—she sits astride my father's shoulders, her legs wrapped around his neck, her body pressed forward, eyes flaming. My father's head is thrown back, his toes grip the sand. Still later—cousin Ellen's wedding, 1973—the whole family is formally posed. I, hugely pregnant, sit alongside Paul and the cousins in the front row, my parents stand with the aunts and uncles in back. My mother has on her winsome public smile. My father is faded and withdrawn. I show the picture to George who recognizes Phil and Gert.

"I've met them several times. Your uncle is a pleasant chap."

* * *

Today is my mother's birthday. Several members of the family send cards. George's daughter sends one too. On a sheet of ecru note paper she has written an affectionate greeting, signed "Warmly, Carol," in parens "George's daughter." I squirrel it into my pocket.

George has been talking about the birthday for days and spending extra time in the ceramics studio. Arriving to chauffeur them to birthday lunch, I find large speckled butterflies on my mother's ears.

"Do I recognize your handiwork, George?"

He smiles widely. "It would be my pleasure to make you a pair, Julia. That is, if they are your kind of thing."

"They are exactly my kind of thing," I lie.

* * *

"So now it's everybody's business." Gert is speaking through clenched teeth. "We might as well put it on the moving letters on Times Square. Can you imagine how I felt when your mother's closest friend, Mollie, whom I have known since before you were born, called to ask if it was true that my sister has a boyfriend? Her husband and your father were best friends all their lives."

"What did you say?"

"I told her my doorbell was ringing. I'd call her back."

* * *

Routines evolve. On Saturdays Carol visits, on Tuesdays I do, making sure each time to clip on the butterflies that I stash in the glove compartment of the car. My mother's disappeared weeks ago. After lunch we painstakingly trek the circumference of the Home, a healthy half-mile, pausing ritually at the base of the gentle incline that leads back to the front doors.

"Here we go, ladies," George announces. "Second gear."

He spends two mornings a week in the studio, experimenting now with watercolors, while my mother rehearses with the Glee Club. On Wednesday afternoons they sit side by side at the weekly Current Events seminar in the Board Room. My mother's eyes move from one speaker to the next, her face seeming to register the full import of the issue being discussed.

Pensive in Paul's arms one night, I shift onto my back and ask, "Do you think my mother and George—?"

He cuts me off. "I don't know, love. I've wondered, too."

* * *

The weather has turned balmy. Dainty tips of daffodils poke through the ground and there are pale buds on every limb. My mother and George sit for hours on a bench near the river, monitoring the gentle traffic of barges and tugs.

With the first draft done, Paul's time has freed up and I am eager for him and George to meet.

"Let's all go out to dinner," I suggest.

"A double-date," he says. "Sounds like fun."

When we arrive, Mom is wearing a fresh spring dress and has taken pains with her makeup.

"Isn't she lovely?" George says.

Rooting about for a comb, I catch sight of the missing butterflies in the corner of a drawer and press them into her hand.

"What are these?" she asks.

"Just put them on," I mutter. "I'll tell you later."

Conversation over dinner is lively but back in the car we are still. Paul takes a lazy, meandering route back. Through the sideview mirror I watch as George draws my mother into the curve of his arm. As she turns into his shoulder I inch a bit closer to Paul. The late spring evening is magical. The trees are lacy with sprouts and soft blossoms. Tulips and lilies are scattered about and the lawns are a soft pea-green. The air is fragrant and summer-still.

* * *

When I arrive this morning, my mother is fussing with odds and ends about her room, wearing the dark blue housedress with tiny dots that she wore, in my mind's eye, every day of my childhood. George is at the window reading the Times. I freeze in the door frame. Inside me a child not older than six stirs brown sugar into a steaming haze of oatmeal.

"Julia, what a surprise. Two days in a row."

"No, Mom, I haven't seen you all week so I drove up for a quick hello."

"What's going on at your house?" she asks.

"Nothing much."

I bend for George's kiss.

"Those earrings look very nice, if I say so myself. How are you?"

"Fine, but things are crazy workwise."

"This is serendipity," George goes on. "Carol is on her way. She will be tied up this weekend so she's coming today instead. Finally you can meet one another."

"When do you expect her?"

He checks his watch. "In about an hour. I said we would be waiting on our bench. It will be a special treat if you can stay."

I think bleakly of the piles on my desk.

Carol waves hello from the window of her station wagon. She's a small woman with a warm, nervous smile. "The tie-ups. Every road into New York is under construction."

I nod commiseratively and for the next few minutes we discuss traffic.

"It's warming up fast," she says. "If you guys are planning a walk, let's take it now."

"Are those shoes comfortable for walking, Syl?" George asks.

"I think so. If they're not, I will just have to lean on you," she says.

George beams. "A dismal prospect."

Fiddling in my bag for the car keys: "I need to go now, Mom."

"You aren't coming to lunch?"

"I'm already late for a meeting. We'll have lunch together next week."

"But I want you to be there now."

"I can't, Mom. I'm sorry." I peck her cheek and flee.

* * *

I find my mother walking listlessly in the corridor today. Her hair is mussed. I doubt that she brushed it or put on lipstick.

"Julia, where have you been? I've been waiting for hours."

"Mom, it's only nine-thirty."

Her mind is elsewhere. "There's a problem with my fella."

My heart freezes. Has George found someone else? No wonder she looks a wreck. "Is George okay?"

"I don't know. He's been missing for a long time."

"Have you checked his room?"

"I may have. I can't remember now. To tell you the truth, Julia, occasionally these days my memory fails me."

"We all have those kinds of days. Come. We'll walk over and see."

"You wait here," she says outside the door. "I'll see if he's home." She peeks in. "He's sleeping," she whispers.

I stare in over her head. Peeping out from the white sheets George looks reduced and vulnerable. I close the door, gesturing my mother into the corridor.

"Why is he still sleeping?" she asks.

"Maybe he had a bad night," I say. "Why don't we walk over to the Board Room and see if there's a lecture going on?"

He has not awakened when I leave.

A few days later I catch my mother hurrying from the dining room.

"Julia, I can't stop to visit. I'm all tied up with a sick friend."

"May I come along?"

"Good idea. Then I can introduce you."

George is sitting up, a breakfast tray pinning him to the bed. "Julia, a pleasure as always."

"Oh, you already know each other," my mother says.

"George, for goodness sake, what happened?"

"I cracked my skull. That's the long and the short of it. We were in the Wellness Center which henceforth shall be known as the Illness Center when I felt a little dizzy and the next thing I knew I was on a stretcher. Apparently I fainted and fell backward onto my head. The doctor has diagnosed a hairline fracture of the skull."

"Is it painful?" I ask.

"Less and less every hour. Your mother is a regular Florence Nightingale."

She holds his hand in one of hers, stroking it lightly. "Enough out of you, mister. You're supposed to be resting."

He nods, "Yes, boss."

* * *

Mom is plainly out of sorts this afternoon. Her costume is a long brown smock with billows of green netting ruffed about the neck. Her face has been cheerfully painted with bright red spots. She is portraying an apple tree in VOICES OF NATURE, the culminating pageant of the combined Riverdale Park Glee Club and the second grade of the local public school.

The din is deafening. Below us, seven-year-olds chase wildly about, careening into chairs and pausing occasionally to shriek full volume into the mike while their teacher yells for attention.

"Julia," my mother says, "I'm so glad to see you. I need help getting out of this sack."

A frail peony peers into her face. "Is this where we're supposed to wait?"

"I don't know," my mother responds. "All I know is that this sack is suffocating. I want to take it off."

"Oh don't," I urge. "It's your costume, so people will see that you're a tree."

"I don't care what they see. I'm all perspired."

"For goodness sake, try to be patient. It's about to begin."

Through superhuman effort the teacher has managed to corral the children into the wings and is painting happy blotches and quizzical lines on their faces. My mother and the peony have been joined on the stage by several other flowers, a moon and a king. The king keeps nodding off, and each time, his cardboard crown slips to the floor, its thud jolting him awake. The moon is knitting to pass the time. Celestial music comes from the tape recorder as the audience files in. I give my mother a good luck squeeze and claim a chair, and then another, as George makes his way to my side.

"I wasn't planning to come again—I saw the dress rehearsal yesterday," he pants, "but Syl seemed so disappointed I changed my mind at the last minute."

I press his hand and then stand, pointing emphatically down at him for my mother to see. But she can't see anything at the moment. She's busy removing her costume as the curtain rises.

It is a triumph. By the final bow, there's not a dry eye in the house. I myself begin to weep during my mother's solo.

"I think that I shall never see/A poem lovely as a tree," she sings, her face soft in the clouds of gauze.

George stares up at her, transfixed. "She sings like Lily Pons."

My eyes are streaming. He pats my arm and hands me a hanky.

My mother is high as a kite afterward. "Did you really like it?" she asks again and again, not this time the repetition of failed memory but of pride.

"Oh yes," I say. "It was wonderful."

"Your solo was the highpoint of the show, no doubt about it," says George.

* * *

The social worker's message is succinct. A situation has developed that she must discuss with me.

"Your mother is fine," she says first off. "The situation involves Mr. Gelman."

George has had another stroke. There are strong indications that he will not regain consciousness. In retrospect, the episode in the Wellness Center was a warning. My mother has been at his bedside most of the morning but he will shortly be moved into the infirmary where only the immediate family may visit.

Turning into George's room, I catch a glimpse of Carol huddled with the staff doctor at the far end of the corridor.

My mother is sitting in a chair by the bed. "Julia, you need to whisper."

I look down at George, my heart knots in my chest, my eyes flood.

"Mom, come out into the hall with me."

"I want to wait until he wakes up," she whispers back.

"Come outside for a minute," I urge.

"That woman looks familiar." She points down the hall toward Carol. "I've seen her before."

"That's Carol, George's daughter."

"Who's?"

"Oh, Mom. George Gelman. Your fella. The man who seems to be sleeping in there."

"Of course he's sleeping," she responds. "Anyone can see that."

I plunge in. "Well, it's not really sleeping."

"What do you mean?"

"Robin called me, Mom. You know, the social worker. George had a stroke. He's very ill."

"He'll be alright soon," she says flatly.

Two aides are wheeling a gurney down the hall.

"I'm going to check on him," my mother says.

"No, you need to wait here."

Robin is heading in our direction.

"They'll wake him up if they move that big thing into his room, Julia. Tell them to stop."

"No, they need to do that. The stretcher will move George to a place where he can get better care."

Robin touches her arm. "Mrs. Freed, let's go up to your room so we can have a little talk."

"Tell them to get out of his room, Julia. He's asleep." Her voice is rising.

"Those men are going to try to make Mr. Gelman better, Mrs. Freed. He's sick now. I'll explain it to you in your room."

"I have to stay here. He's my dearest friend." She stares, appalled, as George is wheeled past us. "I want to go with him."

I reach for her hand—it is icy cold.

"I'm sorry, Mrs. Freed, but only the immediate family is allowed in the infirmary."

My mother looks perplexed.

"Syl, I wonder if you would come along with my father?" Carol is standing behind us.

My mother's face lifts. "Oh," she says. "Yes. Then I can care for him."

Robin raises her eyebrows. "You'll have to assume responsibility."

Carol nods.

* * *

There are about a dozen beds in the infirmary, each enclosed in an oval curtain.

George has been in the coma for twelve days. Tubes are stuck into him, running from a metal arm by the side of the bed. His face has turned pasty yellow. My mother spends most of her time in a chair by his side. Twice a day he is examined by the doctor on staff and occasionally a specialist whom Carol has brought in. Her stationwagon stands every day in the small fenced-in area reserved for infirmary visitors. I drive up every second or third day and cajole my mother outdoors for a brisk walk across the lawns and sometimes a glance into the Board Room.

Finally she has agreed to lunch at the Diner. The waitress greets us like long-lost friends.

"Where's your better half?" she asks my mother.

"Mr. Gelman is ill," I explain.

"Tell him to hurry and recuperate before his pancakes get cold," she instructs, leading us to the corner booth. Sunlight floods in through the broad windows.

"Shall we have the regular, Mom? Pancakes with decaf on the side?"

"Whatever you say."

The orders take forever to arrive. I struggle to maintain the conversational flow. My mother is no help at all. She arranges her napkin meticulously several times and gazes about. When our pancakes arrive I chew extravagantly and signal for the check before the last bite.

"Send Mr. Gelman my best," the waitress calls after us.

"Let's look in at the Board Room before you go back to the infirmary," I suggest. She nods.

A fervent young man is denouncing the federal deficit. We slip into some empty seats in the back row. My mother arranges her face into its full-attention mode. I wait for her urgent hiss, "I need to go back now, Julia," but it does not come.

The instructor ends at fever pitch. Several participants move to the front of the room to continue the discussion, the others drift toward the hall. "I have to get back to the office, Mom."

"I'll walk you to the glass doors. Then I think I'll lie down and catch forty winks."

* * *

Weeding out the used napkins and torn pantyhose from her dresser a few days later, I come upon the butterflies, nested in a corner.

"What are those?" my mother asks.

"Earrings. George made them for you. Remember?"

She turns them over in her hand. "Where did I get them?"

"George made them for your birthday a few months ago. You remember George? Your fella?"

"The name rings a bell," she says.

A late afternoon wind has blown up when I leave and clusters of dry leaves cling to my feet. I glance back at the infirmary where, under muted lights, shadowy figures drift in and out of sight. Then I count up three windows and four across to my mother's room. Her silhouette is barely visible in the window frame. I doubt that she can see me but I wave, just in case.

LIFE LIST

My mother having wandered into Shabbat services at Riverdale Park wearing three blouses and pantyhose, period, her Care Team, meeting in emergency session, ordered an immediate transfer. She is to be moved from the Independent Living Pavilion, home for the past twenty-eight months, into the Alzheimer's Unit, where the support system is more sophisticated and better tailored to her current needs.

It was only a matter of time, I knew. The detailed impersonation of her former self that has played so brilliantly for the past several years is unraveling before my eyes. Her involuntary vocalizing is virtually constant now.

The Alzheimer's Unit is self-contained, that is, locked. The Team has cautioned that in cases like this, where the resident enjoyed considerable autonomy in the Residence and continues to place a high value on her independence, some minor agitation is to be expected, but it will pass.

I call my friend Faith at St. Luke's, where she is recovering from pulmonary surgery, taking a breather, as it were, from her acrimonious divorce from Hal, the sleaze.

"Every time it beeped, the man did you a favor," her friends agreed, a reference to the SmartPhone Hal had fondled in the front row at her father's funeral a few months ago. "Finally, after thirty years, he did something so outrageous it was impossible to ignore."

When she wasn't boxed in business meetings on the 10th floor at Macy's where she is Assistant General Counsel, Faith sobbed continuously after she filed for the divorce. Until eleven days ago, when her internist found the minuscule growth on her left lung that stopped her breath.

"Jule, you sound like death warmed over," says Faith. "What's up? How's your mother?"

The move went badly, I tell her. Robin, the Team social worker, reports that Mom is extremely agitated and needs to be restrained in a therapeutic chair. I hear Faith's muffled voice request that the pills be left on the bedtray, please, along with some water. Then she takes her palm from the mouthpiece and offers warm, loving, sensible wisdom that makes me feel almost whole, for the moment. Also that she has heard that Hal is seeing a shrink.

At Fairway I spot Liane, who works in fiber arts and is going blind, who rose from sitting shiva for her husband who died of AIDS three weeks ago and went directly into the Mobility Training program at the Lighthouse.

"She's strapped into a goddam chair, Liane; it's like the Inquisition," I say.

"You need to calm yourself, Jule. Take a deep breath. Okay? And let it out. Now, let's look at the alternatives here."

"Sedation. The alternative is sedation. You know, medicating her out of her skull, then decreasing the dosage bit by bit. But they warn me that finding the right dosage is tricky and they're concerned that she might fall and break something while they're figuring it out."

As personally she would have trouble tying a dog to a tree, says Liane, she is probably not the best person to discuss restraint. She goes on to offer clear-headed common sense and again, for the moment, I feel calmer. She begs me to borrow her meditation tapes without which she absolutely could not have made it through the past six months. She'll ask her Mobility Trainer to guide her past my house tomorrow and leave the tapes with the doorman.

My daughter calls to report that the firewalk this past weekend had been the peak experience of her life and totally painless except for the tiny singed bits of skin on her sole that had become infected and required debriding in the emergency room.

A month ago, when firewalk hints first popped into her conversation, my mind leapt from stunned to exasperated.

"Must she mortify her flesh to proclaim her selfhood?" I steamed to Faith and Li and anyone else who would listen. "And why is it essential that I know the exact date?"

I tell about Grandma's being tethered to the chair for three days on and off now and she says, "Wow, since Daddy died you've moved into some intense growth period," and also, "Grandma! I mean, the women in this family are something else."

I hang up before something irremediable escapes from my lips.

A note stuck onto the meditation tapes says that first thing in the morning, before sitting down at the loom, works best for Liane. And have I heard from Jeremy lately? The three of us hung out together in graduate school. Also that the Braille is coming along. Killer pun: she always knew she had a feel for languages.

I have not visited my mother since the move, five days now; the Care Team strongly advises that I wait until after the initial adjustment. Meanwhile I flinch every time the phone rings and spend as much time out of the apartment as I can, which is problematical since my computer and fax are there, in my daughter's former bedroom where, under her poster of Thich Nhat Hanh, I write grant proposals for Planned Parenthood. Instead I walk a lot in Central Park—yesterday I spotted a great horned owl etched against the crystalline sky—and also on Broadway, where every few blocks I pass someone who seems a likely candidate for chair restraint.

Every day Robin clocks in with a report from the front. Today's was that things are looking up. The agitation is diminishing. Mom is now able to manage most of the day out of the chair. Also that the dietician on Mom's Team, extension 245, would like a word with me. I phone her up.

During the routine physical exam which is mandatory upon admission to a new unit, the dietician says, the Team found Mom's cholesterol count to be somewhat elevated and has placed her on a low-fat diet. My blood pressure jumps off the charts.

"Are you out of your heads? The woman is ninety years old and demented and you're taking away her ice cream? Give her pastrami, give her omelettes, give her hot fudge sundaes."

The dietician considers that this may not be a good moment and suggests that we speak again shortly.

Robin calls to express her appreciation that I am in touch with my anger about Mom's situation. And would I care to discuss the issue of displacement? A message from Faith: how am I? She's concerned. Who needs Zoloft? Just being at home is a high. It has been recommended that she join an abused spouse support group, either Al-Anon or Gam-Anon. Also, turns out

Hal isn't seeing a shrink as in getting help, he's seeing one as in getting sex. They met at Barnes and Noble ten days ago over a latte. Her name is Batya.

Jeremy calls. His voice is almost back to its normal pitch. The floods are subsidizing. He finally drove his mother back to Leisure Village yesterday. The joys of only-childhood, we know about that.

Having accepted a really great job offer in LA three years ago, Jeremy relocated his widowed mother from her rent-stabilized apartment in Rego Park into Leisure Village, and himself to a condo in the Valley. Between the move, the mudslides, the fires and the floods, his mother's life has been more eventful during the past three years than in all of the previous eighty-seven combined.

Jeremy is into star sightings these days. He keeps a life list. At the Malibu Mall last month he hit the jackpot: Brangelina. Then, "How's your mother doing?" he asks. "What's the tune of the month?"

"It was still The Anniversary Waltz last visit," I begin, "but I haven't been up to see her in almost a week now—" My voice trails off.

"Jule, what's wrong? Tell me what's going on."

So I tell about the move and the chair and how I'm not sure I made the right decision. I should have at least tried to talk them into letting her remain in the Independent Living Pavilion and hired a full-time aide or something. And Jeremy apologizes all over the place for being such a self-absorbed asshole and running on and on about himself. Then he talks for a long time, making any number of quiet points which lead to the conclusion that I made the right decision after all. Did I know, he goes on, that Rudolf Bing lived in the Alzheimer's Unit at Riverdale Park?

I explain that my mother isn't likely to be impressed with Rudolf Bing's name now that she has forgotten her own.

* * *

It's worst at night. My bedroom is filled with thrusts and whinnies and the cracking of wire-tipped crops against raw flanks. I wrench myself from the bedclothes—the dream cowers in the sheets—slip a robe over my shoulders and stare out.

Great chunks of ice lie on the river, pieces of a galactic puzzle, drifting, black as pitch, toward the Bay. Across from me the grim faux fortresses stuck onto the southern tip of the Palisades thrust into the sky. Occasional stick figures stir at illumined half-inches of window. Barges slip silently past.

I need, I need urgently to be held and stroked and told again and again that I am safe. I am a good girl, worthy of love; I need to feel someone else's skin beneath my fingers and my arms and belly, the tangled odors of sweat and breath and come in the twisted sheets. I reach under the flannel gown and knead my arms, my breasts, my thighs. It is insufficient.

The sky is fading. In the thin first light the faux fortresses hang upside down in the shining water. Gulls swoop onto patches of ice, skitter and fly into the pale dawn.

I have not been idle all this time. I have re-examined the current wisdom on the genetic component of Alzheimer's, statistical breakdowns included. And recalled and alphabetized in my mind my daughter's favorite childhood foods and the names of all her grade school teachers. Imagine her surprise to know that some essential part of me admires her sharp need to not accept, to fully experience her life. Will she care for me when I am old?

I have recalled my father's warm whiskery smile, the sheepish droop of his lip, the quiver in my mother's cheek that silenced a classroom. It's gone now, the powerful anger that fueled her relationships over a lifetime, dissolved, vanished, along with the quick wit and passion for the Abraham Lincoln Brigade.

Across the street a red squirrel scoots onto a terrace on the twenty-first floor. How did he land there, so high up, on a frigid night? More to the point, how will he get down?

I can no longer wait. I will visit my mother this morning.

* * *

She is not there when I arrive, clutching a tin of her favorite mixed nuts. The sparse dozen snapshots we together culled from a brimming trunk have been lined up on the bureau facing the narrow bed. Over it someone has posted a sign, WELCOME, SYLVIA. The thin branches of a young magnolia graze the window. Nor is she in the dayroom, where queues of ancient women slump in plastic chairs.

"Try the dayroom one more time," the nurse advises.

This time I make her out. Through the scrim of drugs and bafflement her eyes light. Mine flood over. I bend to kiss her face.

"Come, Mom, let's take a walk."

She strains upward from the chair—it is as if her stuffing has been removed—onto those legs which leapt from the alleys of Minsk to the tenement heaven of East Broadway. Who would ever marry her, my grandparents worried, too fast, always, always in a hurry, too quick, too bright, opinions bursting from her mouth like firecrackers.

"Julia, you were just here yesterday."

She clutches my arm. We shuffle forward.

"You must spend more time at home with your husband. You run too much," she says.

"It's okay, Mom. He doesn't mind."

"I'm thinking of inviting some colleagues over for coffee and cake tonight," she goes on. "Al Shanker promised to drop by."

We pass a beakish hag cackling obscenities.

"I may not include her. Do you think that would be rude?"

"No, Mom. Sensible."

"Good. I'm glad you agree."

Under her breath she sings, "Oh how we danced/On the night we were wed…"

I cut in, startling her, "I needed a wife/Like a hole in the head."

She bursts out laughing. It still works. Deep inside, something releases and my eyes spill out onto her shirtsleeve.

"Oh Mom, it's been a rough couple of days, huh?"

Her grayish hair puffs out around cheeks that to my sure knowledge have known only slaps and pinches for color. Lips whose bareness once implied passion.

"When was it ever easy for the working class?" she replies.

Back in the chair she waves while I fumble for a handkerchief and blow her a kiss. In the car I nibble the nuts. She was not tempted. Next time I'll bring some corned beef.

SANCTUARY

Nora slices right into the driver's mindless breaking-the-ice remarks. "Uh sir, the back seat here is full of dog hair."

"Pardon?"

"Dog hair. All over everything."

"Oh wow. I'm really sorry. Timmy, the dispatcher, handles that. You know, interior vacuuming and all." A chewed Ticonderoga No. 2 behind one ear, beige poly shirt, cranberry-colored pants. "I was sure it was taken care of. Wow."

And this day, with so much tension built in before it even began, slides straight downhill. Shit. How the hell can she hope to unwind in this smelly back seat matted with dog hair? Which was why, rather than trundling up and back in her own perfectly adequate little compact, she splurged on the car and driver in the first place: On-The-Go. Cheapest Rates in the Tri-State Area. $500 for the day up and back, the off-season rate. An extravagance, but aren't all her and Lizzie's friends urging her to take care of herself?

"Stay over," Dan had urged. "Please. It's crazy to go back and forth in one day. You'll be a wreck afterwards. And it's not putting us out in the least. To the contrary, we're eager to have you."

But no, Nora knew that after this punishing day she would need to be at home with the familiar chorizo smells seeping down the hall, the familiar jazz guy upstairs tiptoeing in from his gig, deep under her own feather quilt in her own double bed that seems so enormous these days with Lizzie gone.

"Do you think there might be a whisk broom in the trunk, or a blanket?"

Beep. The driver glances apologetically at his wristwatch. "Sorry." Yanks out the small Poland Spring bottle rubber-banded to the front seat visor, swigs from it, indicates with his chin the trunk of the car. "Only thing back there is the spare. I checked it out, you know, just in case." Lowers his voice. "You might drop a word to John. You know, the boss? I bet he'd knock a couple dollars offa the price."

* * *

While Dan prepares their drinks, the Doberman examines Nora with fierce interest. With his pointed, sticking-up ears, he looks at permanent attention.

Did it hurt when they pinned up your ears that way, fella? I bet. It was Helen, right? That's not Dan's kind of thing. Why'd she go and pin your ears up?

Nora won't ask Dan that question. He's over the moon these days with his new love and his reclaimed lease on life and she must not say a word to cause him self-doubt or concern. Thanks to Helen, Dan has managed to put Lizzie and her illness behind him. Even the difficult daughter, behind him. Lizzie has been dead for eighteen months and now Dan lives in this perfect little bonsai house in Rhinecliff with Helen and the dog, and finally Nora has deigned to visit—more to the point, run out of reasons not to; the snow is gone, even the last vagrant crusts clinging to the side of the road; the head cold that turned into a cough and hung on forever has dried up, too—to meet Helen. To appreciate Dan's amazing good fortune in finding another woman of Lizzie's exceptional quality. Which is impossible, Nora knows. No one will ever measure up to Lizzie.

"One seltzer, slice of lemon," Dan hands her the glass. "How are you, dear? Really?"

An SUV turns into the driveway. Here comes Helen.

"Oh, you know, Dan. Up and down." Nora's voice catches.

Dan comes up behind and kneads her shoulders. "I know. Cleaning out the house was impossible. I mean…I emailed you about the new owners, right?"

"Yeah, I thought about maybe asking the driver to swing by on the way home." She scrutinizes Dan's face which seems to her determinedly impassive. "But snowbirds, you said? That's a lot of house for an elderly couple. And the stairs…"

"They'll make a bundle. Rent it out in the winter months to some yuppie couple with a passel of kids."

A rank, fecund couple rutting away in her and Lizzie's bedroom. It's too much to bear. Her eyes swell.

"We have to let it go, Nora."

"They're not gonna renovate, are they?"

Dan smiles sadly.

Nora recognizes the smile. From the early morning when he lifted Lizzie from the bed into the wheelchair, from when he sponged up the vomit on the kitchen table, from when the doctor said there was no point in continuing the chemo.

Behind the wheel Helen is blotting her lips on a tissue and it occurs to Nora how little she actually knows about her. Is she widowed? Divorced? Are there kids?

The car door slams and a moment later Helen hurries in, busy zipping her tennis-racket back into its case, thrusting her arm forward for a handshake. "Ooh, nippy. Is it really May?" Helen's words tumble hastily one after the other. "I'm glad to finally meet you. I mean, I know it's a cliche. Would you like to use the restroom? I bet you're starved." She shrugs, palms up. "Daniel's told me so much."

Oh yes, definitely she's the pointy-ears type. Nora finds the only smile available at the moment, cheerful, affirming, bogus— and wonders what exactly Dan has told.

How it happened by accident, at the Northeastern Mental Health Professionals annual dinner. More specifically in the womens' room, between courses of baby greens and fennel-encrusted salmon. Every detail must be exact when they're all you've got left.

Lizzie Anshaw, all bangles and gauzy, ethnic layers, rotating her hands under one of those dumb drying machines when Nora charged in, struggling to unbutton the waistband of her black dress-up pant suit. So the first words exchanged were Nora's "Phew, I can breathe again" and Lizzie's amused "Don't I know the feeling." The first lie, come to think of it. Lizzie Anshaw never had to open a tight pant button in her life. Okay, maybe when she was pregnant, maybe then.

Nora was awed, deferential. Lizzie Anshaw was widely admired in the field of domestic abuse. Half an hour before, the entire hall had been on its feet as Lizzie wrapped up a brilliant keynote address. And now here she was, peeing like an ordinary mortal.

A dinner and another, a cluster of late-night phone calls. Eleven years of midweeks together in Nora's rent-stabilized apartment-slash-office, weekends in Beacon, in the sparse four-poster in the guestroom, Dan alone downstairs in the master bedroom, who said he understood. For whom it was not a problem. "We're all grownups here."

Late-day martinis for Lizzie and Dan, a beer for Nora; Saturday afternoon Scrabble which Lizzie always won—"When will you guys finally get that it's about math, not spelling?" Sunday hikes along the river, burly Dan leading the way; over-stuffed Nora; Lizzie crouching in the grass to point out the iridescent turtles crowding the rocks. Stretching toward the hawks overhead.

"Is it true that birds mate for life?" Nora said. "Remember that documentary we saw?"

"Some do." Lizzie laughed. "Hawks and doves. Maybe some others. Swans, I think. But you can bet that fellow"—she pointed to a cardinal pecking at a patch of scrub nearby—"has harems stashed all over the county."

Nora remembered wondering what happened when one of the pair didn't make it through. Was the survivor then fated to be alone for the rest of its life?

One mid-winter weekend Nora arrived to find Dan set up on a futon in the barn; later that evening Lizzie and Nora claimed the master bedroom. Shortly thereafter, his absences began. Four or five hours at a stretch, sometimes longer. One Friday, overnight.

A stony Saturday. Finally, rinsing, drying, stacking after a mostly silent dinner, Lizzie's glacial interrogative: "Staying in tonight?"

Dan's lips tightened. "I beg your pardon?"

"Yesterday you chose to spend the evening out, the entire night in fact, so I thought perhaps…"

"Ah, you would like an official announcement of my plans?"
Things moved quickly downhill from there. Before Nora fled
the kitchen she heard for the first time about the other women.

"Two," he insisted, "just two in thirty fucking years, for
Christ sake."

Murderously, Lizzie inquired, "And now, um, does this make
it three?"

"At this point, I'm not sure that's any of your business," Dan
raged back.

Nora phoned the motel down the road and hastily shoved
her laptop and toiletries into the overnight bag.

"I'll be in that Red Roof just off Route 9," she announced
when finally Lizzie slipped into the room. "And how come—?"

"Shhh. It's all worked out." Mottled color from the argument
still patching her cheeks, Lizzie took Nora's face in her hands
and brought it close, kissed her forehead, the tip of her nose, her
eyelids, as if Nora were a child at bedtime.

Weakly Nora resisted, "I think it would be better…"

Lizzie shook her head. "Leave it alone, my love. It's okay. It's fine."

* * *

Photos line the side hall leading to Dan and Helen's
bathroom: Lizzie on the long breakwater at her family's place at
the beach, baby Chloe in Lizzie's arms even then presenting an
angry face to the world; Helen and two little boys mugging in
Santa Claus hats; a twenty-something Helen with a ponytail, a
husband-type man and a palm tree.

Before they sit down, Dan ambushes her outside of the
bathroom. "Nora, listen—"

"She's lovely, Dan. Delightful. Not that I'm surprised."

"Thanks. I mean. What I wanted to say is…You know, I haven't said anything to Helen about you and Lizzie. I mean, she knows you guys were colleagues and close friends and all. Of course I wouldn't presume to tell you how to handle it but for me…"

"Oh sure. Yeah, I get it."

"Great. Great." He reaches over to squeeze her shoulder. "Terrific."

* * *

Dan seems softer, less opinionated. It turns out to be easy to talk about Lizzie. Even Chloe, the daughter.

"Same old." Dan shrugs. "The point is, she's an adult. When she's ready, I'm here."

Helen works his flannel shirtsleeve with the palm of her hand. "She is always welcome in our home."

Chloe was fucking up at college number three when Nora and Lizzie met. Unshakably, Lizzie held herself responsible. It was Dan who pointed out again and again that Chloe had always been difficult. "From day one. Remember we called her the crib Nazi? Some babies are born that way. It's chemical."

Chloe did not call or visit even once during the terrible last months. A single postcard from Hartford, two hours away. She chose to withhold herself, an ultimate cruelty. Nora doubts that she can ever forgive her.

They've moved onto Dan's painting; Helen is determined that he show in New York next season. It's been too long. She's made the top floor into a studio. "It's Daniel's sanctuary. Completely shut off from the rest of the house. Oh, sanctuary. There's a coincidence. Isn't that the name of the shelter you and

Lizzie set up? What exactly is it? Daniel was involved for a while, right? I mean, are you running it yourself now?"

Dan jumps in before Nora can answer and there is in his tone something so protective, so caring that Nora's eyes fill again. She is unable to respond that nowadays the hours at Sanctuary are the only truly lived ones in her life. Dan tells about her and Lizzie's shared passion, call it imperative, that abused women have a confidential haven in their neighborhood to run to. The preliminary planning, the mission statement, the incorporation as a 501. The daunting ancillary services, counseling, medical, legal that quickly surfaced.

Which brings Nora back to the monthly fund-raising events in her living room. She would be vacuuming like a wild woman when Dan arrived.

"Where'd you park?" she'd yell over the din, poking at the *off* button with her toe. "I mean, it's so kind of you to come all this way."

Dan would shrug uncomfortably, "Here, give me that." Reach for the vacuum. "Damn things weigh a ton."

Moments before the appointed hour, Lizzie would dash in from the clinic clutching cheese, crackers, plastic tumblers, the moisture of the wine bottles imprinted onto the front of her parka. And the all-important guest list, annotated in her firm, backward-leaning scrawl: *long standing int. in womens' issues; time to NAIL; married to major $$$.* Dan and Nora would pore over it in the remaining moments.

The desultory afterwork crowd, mainly friends and their friends, would cluster at the bridge-table-turned bar, settle onto the rented chairs as Lizzie moved through the room hugging, exclaiming. From her station at the door Nora would watch, giddy with pride, as Lizzie quickly clapped her hands for quiet, then introduced Dan.

Backlit at the window, Dan would describe the realities of domestic abuse, the entrenched cycles handed down generationally, the violence no doubt occurring as he spoke. Energy would stir. Passionate now, he would build to the possibilities, the plan. Checkbooks were brought forth, funding proclaimed. The crowd was roused, galvanized.

Afterwards, over dinner at the Greek place on the corner, Nora and Dan reported jubilantly, interrupting one another, filling in, while Lizzie scribbled notes on the crumpled guest list. Then Lizzie and Dan headed home to Beacon while Nora trudged alone back to the apartment, dispatched the soiled napkins, refrigerated the rest of the cheese, crawled into the wide double bed, the only tangible reminder of Ellen, her grad school roommate, her first partner.

The night before, she and Lizzie would have lain awake strategizing, their toes working tiny puckers into the bottom of the sheet until Nora groaned, "Okay, enough."

"I know but wait—" Always Lizzie had more to add. Nora would plaster her palms over her ears, "Abuse, abuse." Lizzie would wrestle them off, both of them shrieking, tousling, breathless, quieting down, reaching out for one another in the dark.

"Someone comes in part-time to handle the clerical stuff," Nora manages.

"Me, I'm just a stayed-at-home Mom," Helen declares.

Dan grouses that he hates it when she sells herself short like that. "What about the literacy project? The canvassing?"

Helen demurs and changes the subject. "How was the ride up?"

Nora's mind is still floating.

"Nora?" Helen prods, her voice rising a notch.

"Oh. Sorry." Quickly Nora switches gears. "Fine. It's great looking out the window while someone else drives."

"We know about that." Helen nods, woman to woman, and purses a kiss to Dan.

Nora describes the streaming willow hairs, the coiled purple skunk cabbages, the tulip shoots, editing out Lizzie's flat, funny insistence that if you really listened you could hear the buds pushing through the soil.

In fact, Nora thinks, if she hadn't come, she might be peering through the kitchen window at this very moment, monitoring the tiny tulip sprouts in the park. No, the truth is, she'd be online chatting with Voltage or Mewoman, her new best friends, on the Internet Scrabble site to which she has become seriously addicted, who know only that she is female and from New York, with a tendency to fold when the board gets tight.

"Is he still sitting outside?" Helen asks. "The driver? I mean, should I invite him in for some lunch?"

"No, no. He'll fend for himself. I've got his cell number for when I'm ready to leave. Actually he's a character."

She tells about the dog hair—"Shame on them, do you want me to have a word with the owner?" Dan inserts—and the hourly beeps. "After beep number three—we were on route 9 by then—I asked what the deal was. His chiropractor said to watch his hydration. They're a reminder to take another swig."

Dan rolls his eyes.

Silence follows. A squirrel scratches in the soil outside the kitchen door. In the distance, a horse knickers softly, a chain-saw grinds. The sun slips quietly through the long afternoon toward the hills, rays filtering through the large screened-in porch.

Dan clears. "No, no. You sit right there. You're a guest. Next time, which will be soon, you get to help." He italicizes the "soon."

Nora smiles and nods and leans down to pat the poor, maimed puppy, glances at her watch. Whispering from the kitchen. They're talking about her. Of course. Wouldn't she?

"Nora, there's Cherry Garcia and Choca Mocha," Helen calls, "but they're hard as rocks because naughty Daniel forgot to take them out of the freezer. Coffee in the meanwhile?"

Nora yells back Lizzie's trick. "You might try sticking them in the microwave for a moment."

* * *

The day is fading and the peepers are out now, their high ecstasy filling the air. A blue jay rasps its mating cry, a dove coos. The majesty of northern Dutchess gives way to the gentler river towns: Carmel, Cold Spring, Beacon where Lizzie and Dan and toward the end Nora, lived, in the white colonial on Colton Drive, down the road from Norman Mailer's ex. Nora can never remember which ex. Not the one involved in the stabbing. Across from the Johnstons' farm, one of the few working farms in the county.

The Johnstons board horses. That last fall, Nora would wheel Lizzie down the road in the afternoon and deep into the horse pasture, the wheels catching on the pungent thyme weeds. Lizzie had stopped wearing the scarf to cover up the growing-in patches of fuzz on her scalp. Dan was disappearing routinely for four or five hours at a stretch. Overnight, occasionally. If Lizzie noticed, and of course she did—the woman missed nothing all her too-short life, nothing—she chose not to remark. The thought came afterward to Nora: was that Helen? And later still; who cares?

As they came down the path, a pinto, bold splats of brown fur over white, would move toward them, smelling her lapful of fresh mint which she would feed to him handful by handful, kneading his long nose with the heel of her hand. Then they would sit, Nora plucking at the grass, hugging her knees, leaning her head sideways onto the high metal wheels of the chair as the horses moved about them, switched their tails, trembled the pesky flies from their backs. A filly might toss and flip over, hooves flying, chafing her back into the grass. The others would pass without a glance, winnowing softly, pawing the rosemary that blanketed the meadow this time of year. Reflexively Lizzie's hand would reach out to Nora, to just under her hairline where the muscles permanently cramped with stress, and Nora would lean full, grateful weight into her fingers.

What was Lizzie thinking about, Nora would wonder. Chloe? Sanctuary? At the time she, Nora, hadn't thought about anything beyond the absolutely concrete: how long after the potatoes should she start the green beans? Should she set the table for two or three?

Even later, under the quilt, Lizzie's body curved around hers in a casual C (to the end she remained the protector, the shelterer from the storm), when Nora could no longer shut out the inevitable: no Lizzie in the world, Lizzie terminally gone, and she would bite down on the soft skin between her thumb and forefinger to keep from crying out, Lizzie kept silent.

The beeping is gone, at Nora's request, and after half an hour Cranberry-Pants asks if it's okay to make a pit stop. Big surprise, buddy, with all the water you've pumped into yourself. No, just keep on driving. Who cares if you piss your pants? Not my problem. Which, in case you're interested, is that my partner, my lover, the crucial person in my world, is dead and now her husband is re-attached to a woman who pinned her dog's ears up. But "Sure," she says. "I'm ready for a stretch." And before she knows it, there is a 7-11 and Cranberry-Pants hustles across the parking area while Nora walks to the far end and stretches her arms upward.

A Morgan stallion arches elegantly in the wide field adjoining the lot. Nearby, a goat grazes alongside the fencing. Horses and goats. Who would have thought? And the real question, which has been half-hidden in her mind all day: should she stop and see the house? It's so close, two exits down and only half a mile off the road. Who knows when next she'll find herself here?

But no, it will have changed. The perennial bed will be overgrown, barely recognizable, the beautiful side porch crammed with portacribs and strollers or even, God forbid, lopped off; skylights will be slashed into the living room ceiling—and that will be awful. Or maybe not, maybe it will be exactly the same, the peonies preparing to turn gorgeous, the white wicker chairs on the side porch overhung with red and pink fuchsia, cruelly seductive, and that will be even worse.

Cranberry-Pants is hustling back toward the car, his head darting in anxious jerks as it becomes apparent that Nora is not in the back seat. She waves largely from across the lot—he hasn't lost her.

Back in the car, Nora tugs at the blanket that Helen insisted she take, and a pillow too. Unnecessary, as it turned out. During the long afternoon, Cranberry-Pants has thoroughly washed and vacuumed the car, which smells mildly now of scented detergent. Of course she thanked him, though with scant enthusiasm. Why could she not accept his gift with grace? When will her heart open again?

A clutch of turkeys shambles through a ditch beside the road. And oh, up ahead where the video store used to be, an honest-to-goodness strip mall has sprung up. Radio Shack, Dunkin' Donuts, CVS. Tick Tock—their favorite diner—has been replaced by a sushi palace.

No, there's no need to see the house. Just as well she hasn't mentioned it to the driver. It's old news, history. Maybe sometime years from now, if she finds herself up in this part of the world, she might drive over to see it for old times' sake.

Nora pulls the pillow behind her head, yawns, her eyes drowse over. The car tires thrum on the pavement. The peepers are bolder now, blanketing the air.

ROSIE

AT THE MOMENT SARAH is lying in Spokane General, struck ten days ago by a viral paralysis which, the doctors assure us, will reverse itself in time.

Rosie, her four-year-old, is here with me in New York. How she came to be here is a long story. Arthur is behind his monumental desk overlooking Wall Street and we are speaking to one another on the telephone with grim cordiality.

He notes that Rosie has been in New York for three full days and he has not yet seen her; therefore, his wife, the fulsome Phyllis, has invited us, Rosie and me, to dinner tomorrow night. I respond, with cunning use of the conditional, that Rosie having had to cope with so many new situations in the past few weeks, it might make more sense for us all to have dinner at my apartment, which is somewhat familiar. Ah, but Phyllis has already invited a neighbor from downstairs with her little girl so that Rosie will have someone to play with.

"Arthur, listen, I'm not sure that what Rosie needs right now is a new friend. I think maybe she needs familiarity and to feel safe."

"Vintage Lucy," says Arthur. "Always got that third ear cocked. And look where it's landed you. Not to mention Sarah."

Which gives you a clue as to why I finally left him. But I will not back down. When it comes to Rosie I am a force of nature.

"So let me get this straight," Arthur goes on. "The phone rings in the middle of the night and it's this Harry guy and he says he needs a round-trip ticket to New York plus a one-way ticket for Rosie and they arrive two nights ago and he drops her and takes off."

I had swum upward toward the ringing. It was the hospital, I knew. Who else would call at that hour?

"Lucy, it's me."

"Avi. What's happening?"

Through the sheets Michael reached for me.

"Nothing, nothing. No change with Sarah yet. I'm sorry to wake you so early but Lucy, I am having a problem here and you offered—"

It poured out in a sorrowful recitative that reduced to Rosie's refusal to go to daycare or to visit with her little friends and the impossibility for Avi to return to work with her at home.

"The principal has been great—I had to miss all the meetings—but my classroom is barely set up and the kids come back next week."

The telephone cord unwound to its farthest loop as I spooned back into Michael. Of course, then Rosie must come and stay with me for however long and Avi must not feel guilty, a change of scene might be good for Rosie once she had settled in, and he would be free to work and to visit Sarah in the evenings.

"I'll tell them this morning that I need to be away again. The Labor Day week is slow at the Institute in any case. I'll plan to fly out tomorrow."

"No, no," Avi insisted. "I will bring her to New York. The flight is exhausting and you just got back a few days ago. Besides," he went on, "it will make a smoother transition for Rosie."

After the call I nuzzled into Michael's chest hairs. "Probably makes sense for you to sleep at your place for the first couple of days."

"How long do you think she'll be here, anyway?" He puffed his cheeks in vexation. "Shit. Forget I said that, okay?"

Five nights later—Rosie had arrived that day—I was awakened by a thin cry—"Sarah, Sarah," I called thickly, "I'm coming"—followed by a full-blown wail. I pitched into full wakefulness and snatched Rosie from the cot at the foot of the bed tight onto me.

"It's okay, lovey, it's okay, you're here with me, with Grandma. See. Here's your pillow from home. And your blanket. Avi packed it in the suitcase for you."

Half-asleep, face hidden from me, she muttered, "You don't know. It's not my blanket, it's my quilt."

* * *

This is the longest dinner in the history of the world.

Phyllis's current diet requires that she chew every bird-mouthful twelve times. So to my right Phyllis's mouth is roto-rootering away and she's only halfway through her entree and believe me she's not about to leave a single edible morsel on her plate because God knows when she's allowed to eat again.

Arthur and I have been finished for a mute twenty minutes—at the moment we are unable to talk civilly to one another—and you can bet I have discouraged Phyllis from conversation. Rosie left the table a week and a half ago to watch The Pigs' Wedding, her current favorite video. As she was climbing down off the high-back dining room chair Arthur asked if she would like to be excused.

When they arrived, he had leaned down and handed her an immense and gorgeous doll from France with its own make-up valise, and when Rosie said "Thank you Grandpa" which we had rehearsed, his eyes welled up. Phyllis asked what the doll's name would be and Rosie said Skye and then she said she meant Skye-Phyllis and Phyllis's exquisitely shadowed eyes welled, too.

"She's a dream," she mouthed to Arthur.

While I made the drinks Phyllis piled Rosie's fine yellow hair on top of her head and taught her the difference between a French braid and a French knot.

"So let me make sure I have this 100%." Majestically, Arthur clears his throat. "This Ari guy is not Rosie's father."

"His name is Avi. 70%."

Arthur's eyebrows ask Phyllis if she sees what he means. "How can you be so sure?" he returns.

"Because Sarah said so. She knew we'd make that assumption."

"But he was willing to fly all the way from Spokane to New York to bring her here and then turn around and fly right back? The guy must be crazy." He adds, "Or someone is lying."

Rosie sways toward the table now, reverently, the way one does when cradling a new baby. Only this doll looks peculiar in a cradling position. It's easier to picture it smoking a cigarette.

"Grandma, did you say Avi's name? I need to talk to him." She hands up the doll to me, clambers after it.

"Lovey, he always calls when he finishes working. It's just four o'clock in Spokane. Pacific time. Remember?"

"But I have to tell him something. Now." Her brow tightens with emphasis. "It's important."

"Try to be patient."

"Then maybe I can call my Momma," Rosie continues. "Maybe it's all right to talk to her today."

Arthur leans forward. "Would you like to tell me the important information?"

Rosie's thumbnail picks at the raw inner pad of her index finger. "It's a secret."

"A secret," coos Phyllis. "I love secrets. But I never before had a little girl to share them with. Shall I tell you a secret?"

"Oh yes." Rosie is enchanted. She scrambles around the table and cocks her ear into Phyllis's voluminous bosom.

"I love you," Phyllis stage-whispers.

Rosie's face goes all noodly. "Me too," she whispers back.

"Would you like to come home with Grandpa and me and sleep in our extra bedroom?"

"Oh." Rosie is overwhelmed. "Is there a DVR?"

Phyllis nods and crinkles up her features. Her eyes find Arthur's.

"And maybe in the morning we can go to the museum," Phyllis continues, "where they have big dinosaurs. And maybe the next day we can go to the zoo."

"The zoo," Arthur trumpets. "Sounds like fun to me." His voice resumes its normal pitch. "Are you almost done with that chicken, Philly?"

Phyllis returns to the job at hand.

My voice is gritty, close to the edge. "Run and play, lovey, I'll call you for dessert."

But Rosie is not ready for dismissal. "Grandma, I saw a scumbag out the window. A fat lady scumbag. She threw a candy wrapper right on the sidewalk. I yelled scumbag but I don't think she heard me."

"Probably not. We're way up on the tenth floor." My fingernails drum a tattoo on the tablecloth. "Rosie, would you run into my bedroom, please, and see if I left my glasses there? Look really hard. I need them."

I use the moment until she is out of earshot to place my tone. "That is such a generous invitation, Phyllis, but I'm not sure that tonight is the best time for a sleepover. You know, Rosie just got here and things are still a bit confusing for her. Could we plan it for sometime later?"

Arthur's eyes are dancing see-what-I-mean again. "What makes you think she's confused? She doesn't sound confused." He leans full weight into the back of the chair. "I am her grandfather, after all. I'd like her to feel at home in our place, too. I mean, you never know."

"What? You never know what, Arthur?"

The sound of bicuspids mashing chicken is the only one in the room.

At my side Phyllis is piling chicken bones into a teepee on her salad plate. Above us the inharmonious scrapings of chair legs against hardwood floors; my upstairs neighbor is clearing the table with the kids. His wife must be working late.

"So the neurologists promise no residual aftereffects?"

"Well, they're not about to engrave it in stone, Arthur, but the percentages are very much in Sarah's favor."

Silence.

"While we're at it, Lucy, let me check Sarah's address here." Cards stream from Arthur's wallet to the tablecloth. "The damn post office returned both cards we sent." He seizes one. "Lawton Avenue, isn't that it?"

"It was. She and Avi moved over a year ago."

"No one let me know." Aggrieved silence. "I can't believe that no one bothered to tell me where my own daughter was living."

My tone is flat. "I don't think she knew you would care."

"What's that supposed to mean?"

"That you have been in touch with Sarah only once since Rosie was born."

"It's been a difficult period, communication-wise," Arthur growls. "Philly, why don't you ask Lucy to wrap that last piece of chicken and take it home? I mean, for Christ sake."

Phyllis offers a placating smile.

"So. If this Harvey person isn't Rosie's father, then who the hell is? Did you ask her that?"

Of its own volition my chair screeches backward from the table.

"Arthur. Sarah has been clear from the beginning. As you know, she will not declare Rosie's biological father. She plans to raise the child alone."

"But apparently she didn't plan on becoming paralyzed so the plan has changed, am I right?"

Had I mentioned that Arthur is a litigator?

Here comes Rosie on the double, her two middle fingers extended in a fat V. "No glasses, Grandma, I looked really hard. But three more scumbags."

"Shame on them," I cluck. "Messing up the city."

Phyllis has set her knife and fork onto the plate, barren now except for the bones, and beckons Rosie to her lap.

"Now Grandma Phyllis wants you to tell her a secret," she whispers.

I pause midway to the kitchen.

"Grandma Phyllis wants to know what a scumbag is."

"Don't you know? Everyone in Spokane knows." Rosie's face gleams with zeal. "A scumbag is a human who litters and makes the world bad for other humans."

"She doesn't sound confused to me," remarks Arthur.

"I'm four," Rosie says.

"Oh, it's a litterbug," says Phyllis. "Litterbug is such a pleasant word. It's humorous."

"So is scumbag huminous," Rosie returns.

Arthur leans in. "Rosie, because you love Grandma Phyllis, could you try very hard to say litterbug instead?"

"Places, everyone," I yell from the kitchen. "Dessert is served." Rosie's tough-face is on as she scrapples back onto her chair.

Arthur trudges the five or six steps back and forth to the kitchen, helping to clear. His whole face sags gently south. He could not suck in his paunch now if he tried. The deep sadness that I have always sensed in him is palpable.

In the living room Phyllis is demonstrating highlighting techniques on Skye-Phyllis, who radiates new and stunning amazements every time I look. Her eyes have been blue and green and hazel thanks to microscopic contact lenses. Her hair has been frizzy and buttery smooth. At the moment it is being permed.

"I don't recall Sarah ever playing with dolls." Arthur's voice is mild.

"She didn't much. She was always poking around in the yard or the lots in back."

Arthur has perched on the kitchen stool, his fifty-eight year old butt lopping over the edges. He shifts onto one cheek. "Westchester feels like a dream," he says. "If we had stayed in the city, do you think she would have gotten so hooked on playing in the mud?"

"Botany, Arthur," I say absently. "Sarah is a botanist."

"Whatever. I used to wonder if she'd bother to scrub her nails for her wedding. Now I'll never know."

"Know what?" I've lost the thread, my eyes glommed onto Phyllis in the next room. "She's not that bad" is the unwelcome reality inching into my mind.

Arthur's voice hauls me back. "What's happening with your father?" he asks kindly.

"Riverdale's an excellent Home. One of the best, everyone says. But he's so changed." The chrome of the dishwasher is cool against my bare legs. "Some days he's almost mellow."

"Your father, mellow? Now there's an oxymoron."

"I know, I know. He was a difficult guy. Where did it come from? His parents were the sweetest souls." Pure pleasure washes over me. "When I was young they lived just under us. My grandma used to let me hide my overdue library books behind her sewing machine."

"I barely remember her. Maybe a vague memory of her funeral but that's it." Above us a pair of high heels clacks, a kettle is placed, a kitchen drawer slams shut. The wife is home. God, I miss Michael. Rehearsal must be over. Is he home yet? Has he changed into his sweats?

Arthur gestures toward the living room. "She's some kid."

"And Sarah's a terrific mother. I'm proud of her."

"I don't know about this alternate life-style garbage. God knows I tried to talk sense to her when she got pregnant. But if it works for them—" His tone shifts. "And you?"

"Okay. More than okay. I'm fine. You know, working and loving."

"Great. I see the Institute mentioned in the paper all the time. Is that musician guy still hanging around?"

"Michael. His name is Michael."

"Yeah, Mike." He shifts.

My kitchen is back to normal. Sheer humidity seeps through the open window. The tiny peat pots that Rosie and I planted this morning are lined up on the ledge like a dwarf militia: leaf lettuce, peas, dill, cherry tomatoes, arugula.

On the coffee table Skye-Phyllis, wearing a negligee that I wish I owned, is stretched out on my Belgian lace runner while Rosie and Phyllis squirt body lotion onto her fake-skin limbs and smush it around. Phyllis has lost her high sheen. Her lipstick is mostly eaten off. Her bare arm brushes Rosie's cheek and lingers.

"Now her vulva. She needs some lotion on her vulva." Rosie hikes the negligee toward the doll's middle.

My head jerks up. Phyllis's face looks as if it has been spat on.

"Come on, you need to do your side," Rosie instructs. Poor Skye-Phyllis lies all askew, her flimsy nightdress hitched up halfway.

"I think she has enough lotion. Definitely enough lotion. Her skin looks nice and smooth." Phyllis calls out to the kitchen, "Don't you think so, Lucy? Grandpa?"

Arthur's right eye has gone peculiar. "Smooth as silk. Absolutely smooth as silk." He sounds extremely convinced.

"No, she needs some on her vulva, like my Momma did for me when I ate eggs and got a rash there. Mmmm, it felt wonderful. It took the itching right away."

Phyllis's wrist flaps over onto its side. "Oh my, look at the time. That doll should have been in bed hours ago. She needs her beauty sleep."

"No," says Rosie, "It's early. She's on Pacific time."

At which point I march into the living room. "It's time to put the doll away, lovey. Have you watered your plants yet this evening?"

Everything begins moving at once, Rosie churning into the kitchen, Phyllis wobbling down the hall toward the bathroom, Arthur striding toward the front hall closet. Rosie returns clutching a peat pot—Burpee Deluxe Cherry Tomato. Hoists herself into the wing chair. Arthur, weighted with Burberrys, turns to her and stops short. Balled into a corner she is busy drooling beads of saliva into the peat pot, the miniscule muscles under her chin pulsing her tongue back and forth to maintain the flow. He shifts abruptly, intercepts Phyllis in mid-hall and swerves her from the living room toward the front door, at the same moment slipping the coat over her shoulders.

"I'll phone you about that sleepover," Phyllis coos in the doorway.

Arthur says to let him know when I hear anything new about Sarah. I give it one serious shot.

"Rosie, put down that peat pot for a minute and come say goodnight to Grandpa and Phyllis."

But she is totally consumed in the creation of an elongated strand of drool.

"Goodnight dear," they call toward the living room. In turn they kiss my cheek and flee.

* * *

Four days have gone by. Yesterday a book arrived from Barnes and Noble—you-know-who and the Knights of the Round Table—with a note signed Grandpa that said it was his favorite story when he was Rosie's age and he'd stop by on the way home from work one night soon and read it to her. We haven't heard yet from Phyllis.

Rosie has made it all the way through three nights in a row. Cause for celebration, though I have warned myself to expect some backsliding. Michael came back yesterday, carrying a pair of mice in a cardboard box with holes punched in the lid. After dinner we all three did the dishes, then Michael and Rosie watched The Pigs' Wedding while I did blessed nothing for half an hour.

Avi's nightly phone call is the fixed point in our lives. Sarah has begun to feel sensation in her limbs and in a few days she will be helped to sit up. Since that bulletin Rosie has been turning out art works at a phenomenal rate. She is making a special book for Sarah.

I have never been so tired in my life. At the moment we are poured like syrup, Rosie and I, in tank tops and shorts, on the Barcalounger. She is lying full on top of me, our toes wiggling companionably, like stubby old friends having a gossip. A frayed band aid is peeling from her big toe, where I had extracted a splinter last night.

The bedroom is filled with silence. Rosie's divine baby butt is moored on my knees. Her head reaches to just under my breasts and from there her amazing cornsilk hair fans up and out and over my shoulders.

BLAUSTEIN'S KISS

BEN BLAUSTEIN OPENS THE door of his room. Wearing a fresh shirt and the pants from his High Holy Days suit, which hang long onto his shoes even though the waist is hitched up with suspenders. Today darling Meryl will come. His beloved Ceil's daughter. Sometime in the next hour perhaps. Hour and a half, tops. He felt it the moment his eyes opened. Over a lifetime one learns to respect these instincts.

"Ah, Mr. Blaustein, good morning." Ms. Campos at the nurses' station holds out a paper cup. "The meds."

Game Time. He tucks the paper under his bad arm and dodders over. Gazes at the cup.

"For what?" Elaborately Blaustein shrugs.

"La corazon." Ms. Campos pats her ample bosom.

Blaustein permits his gaze to linger. She holds out the next cup. A white pill. Again he shrugs.

"For the bones." She clenches a fist in the air. The tip of a beige nicotine patch is visible under her sleeve.

"And last..." A gigantic capsule, that reaches almost to the top of the cup.

Another shrug.

"To soften the stool."

He waits, eyes teasing, until this time she shrugs. He smiles. Two years and she still hasn't come up with a gesture for that one.

Cautiously he tightens his grip on the paper cup of water. He must be careful not to let it slip like the other time.

"What's going on with the children?" he asks, although he knew instantly this morning, from the tight-strung cords at the back of her neck, to expect a bad report.

"Last night my Dalia opened her mouth to me, like the devil has taken her."

Her eyes are swimming, poor thing. Blaustein pats her arm. Always there are problems, and if it involves schooling he may offer advice, but lately the issues are ones of limits and generational respect. All too familiar. His own Lena gave him and his wife a good run for their money. Ms. Campos would find that reassuring, he thinks. He must tell her. But maybe he already has. Better to say nothing. He must be on guard for slip-ups like that.

The whole topic of Ms. Campos and her children seems suddenly monumentally complicated. It would take a major effort to continue the line of thought and at the moment he's not up to it. He feels the energy seeping downward from his brain. Once more he touches Ms. Campos's arm, the one without the patch—which reminds him, he must commend her for trying again—and slowly turns his shoulders from the station. His favorite chair, the one with the long view down the corridor, is still vacant, thank goodness. He nods cordially to Faygel Stein in her wheelchair—now she is silent but when she did speak it was always about her parents—the magnificent bakery, the rugelach, the mandelbrot—settles himself and opens the newspaper.

"But my Times?" he fretted when Lena first brought up the move. She reassured him in that awful, infantilizing tone she has taken on since her mother passed away.

"You'll open the door in the morning and voila, it will be waiting for you. I keep telling you, Dad, it's not just lip service. At Riverdale, they care about those things."

Who are they? he wondered. And why should they give two figs for his newspaper?

The corridor is empty except for the isolated nurse or aide but now at the far end a group from the outside world appears, craning anxiously. An orientation tour. Probably Meryl is trapped somewhere in there. Or just behind, her step slowed by the crowd. He can sense her wry impatience, the amusement just under her eyes, all so like her mother's, rest in peace. Certainly she would never shove her way through. She is her mother's daughter: gracious, cultivated.

He remembers his orientation tour, Lena tailing behind with the other grown-up children, before the final decision to move in. That was when he found out about sharing a room.

"But I taught for forty years in the classroom, in the early years also in night school, to put aside funds for my daughter's education and my wife's old age and my own, and now I am not permitted even one room to myself?" he screamed silently, blinking without sight at something the social worker was pointing to. His eye caught Lena's face, dissolved. This she had been unable to tell him.

But it had been a good decision. Cautiously he involved himself in the life of the community—the Residents' Council, the Intergenerational Chorus, and there, in the front section reserved for short and/or near-sighted people—Blaustein was both—he met Ceil. Also short and near-sighted. And genteel and lively and surprisingly warm. Surprising even to herself. And ironically, although his Times waits every single morning without fail, these days he feels less and less inclination to read it, to follow with his magnifying glass line after line of hypocrisy and heartache. The truth is, he will not be around to know the ending to these awful stories.

In the two months since Ceil passed away, rest in peace, the world has gone crazy. Terrorists, chemicals. The residents were issued special gloves to open their mail. The latex fought him—it took twenty minutes to get the glove onto one hand. He tossed them aside. At ninety-one, does it matter if he dies of anthrax or pneumonia?

And now he is crazy too. Crazy for the swell of Ceil's flesh against his in the narrow bed, for the nudge of her nipple in his palm, the wetness between her legs. It was not easy but with persistence he could still snake a finger down past the elastic of her panties into the wetness and then up again to his lips. Nectar of the Gods.

"Leave off the panties," he begged. "Please. Who will know?"

She shook her head. Some things were too much to ask.

His penis curled in her palm. It had taken weeks to persuade her but finally, with his hand guiding, she reached down and found it with her fingertips. Heaven. She cupped it gently, still stroking. Double heaven. Like a mouse, Ceil laughed softly. Or a hamster. Her daughter, Meryl, had kept one for a pet. Imagine, a kosher hamster. They giggled like children. Ceil pressed her mouth into his shoulder to stifle the sounds. In the next bed Lazar, the roommate, groaned aloud in his sleep. It had not ever been like this with his wife. Blaustein had taken the initiative as he should. Eventually she came to enjoy it. Or so she said.

But this was ardent and ever-present. In the Wellness Center he chose a spot behind Ceil so he could watch her buttocks tensing each time her ankle kicked forward. At the Sunday concerts he pressed his arm into her breast.

* * *

At her desk on Columbus Circle, Meryl is thinking about Ben Blaustein. His tongue, specifically. Poking past her clenched lips into her mouth. And his hand grazing her breast. Her whole body contracts in disgust. She looks up past the spreadsheet on her screen to be sure her office door is shut, exhales and reaches for the phone.

The number is permanently programmed into Meryl's fingers; how many times over the year has she called Ms. Campos? Her mind shifts back to the winding down moments of her mother's first day. Her parents' formal wedding photo was angled on the chest in her half of the room. Tucked into the frame, obliterating a piece of pastel sky, two snapshots: Meryl, squinting under the Law School mortarboard, and two little girls squealing from a bathtub, their hair shampooed into foaming teepees. Her mother's bathrobe hung from a hook in the shared bathroom. The roommate had not yet appeared. Perhaps she was giving them some privacy while they settled in—a hopeful sign.

"Okey-doke, you're fired. Go on home." Her mother turned from arranging her everyday jewelry in a compartment of the top drawer. "Kiss the girls for me." Softly, "Honey, what would I do without you?"

Was this the drill, was she now expected to walk away, leaving her mother alone. Her eyes filled, she slipped into the hallway. Ms. Campos had come up behind her then. Guided her toward the console. Handed her a tissue and the number for the nurses' station, on a piece of paper torn from a prescription pad.

"Call when you need to," she said. "Don't worry, I'll be here all night. If your mother is awake, I'll bring her the phone." That was a lifetime ago.

"Ms. Campos, it's Meryl, Ceil's daughter. Ceil Koven? Fine, fine. And you?" Meryl runs a hand through her overgrown blunt cut.

Ms. Campos's responses are crisp, monosyllabic. Meryl appreciates the tone, practical, not unfriendly.

"Ms. Campos, I called because I'm concerned about Mr. Blaustein. I mean, I wondered. Has there been some adjustment to his meds?"

Meryl's secretary buzzes. She places a hand over the mouthpiece. "Take a message, please." Removes it. "Yes, I'm still here. Sorry. I was wondering. The last few visits he..." This is impossible. "Onto my breast, yes. And his tongue kept..." Meryl struggles to find the words, specific but non-judgmental, to describe Ben's lechery. "Yes, I did warn him. Three times. I laid down ground rules. Damn, I feel like I'm tattling to the principal."

Ms. Campos expresses her gratitude that Meryl has made her aware of the situation. "This must be very difficult for you." She will speak with Mr. Blaustein's social worker immediately.

Meryl replaces the phone, stares out the window. Ben, courtly, delightful Ben, who transformed her mother's last year, whom Meryl also adored. The whole mess feels unreal. Her view north over the park is comforting. The bridge gleams in the distance. And the sixth floor is exactly right: plenty of sky but low enough to feel the vibrations of street life. Which reminds her that she hasn't made it to the gym in months. The zipper of her pants are strained to the limit. Now a squirrel scrambles into view, leaps to another branch. Oh Ben. She would not be shocked to look out and find him perched on a limb, peering over his newspaper into her office.

He was her mother's final bequest. Her eyes gripped Meryl's on that long last morning. She moistened her lips with her tongue, murmured, "Afterwards dear, when you can, run up to see Ben." Her eyes closed, re-opened. With effort she worked her lips. "This will be hard on him."

Meryl nodded. Her mother's face was the only reality. Everything else: the metal pole from which the tubes hung, the yellow curtain pulled to the side, the bed itself, were unfamiliar, alien.

"He likes dried fruit, especially..." Her mother's voice trailed off.

Ben was not expected at the funeral, his own health fragile at best. But before the service, from the sofa in the jammed anteroom where Meryl sat with the two girls and her aunt—even her ex-husband was there—she spotted him, Lena by his side, plodding forward, his round face under the yarmulke all crumpled.

"Oh Ben, you should not have come."

"He was insistent," Lena whispered. "The doctor felt it might be more harmful if she forbade it."

"That it is difficult, Meryl, is no reason not to come. I loved Ceil. I owe her this respect and you as well." He listed precariously. "I wonder if I might sit for a moment."

There was a time early on in their parents' courtship when she fantasized that she and Lena were sisters—each an antidote to the other's only-childness—carrying together this burden of their aging parents. Often then they planned their visits to coincide, grabbing a quick bite afterward.

But over the months, as Meryl's case load grew, it made sense for her to visit early in the day. Too early for Lena's drive in from the suburbs. So early that one morning she found her mother and Ben curled together in his bed. There they lay, like antique spoons. Heirlooms. Ben puffed peacefully through his half-open mouth onto her mother's hair. Meryl shook her head in wonderment—they looked so perfectly right—and drew the door behind her.

Ms. Campos looked up from the nurses' station. "The pastry in the coffee shop is not too bad."

* * *

Lunchtime. Still no Meryl. A complication at the office, no doubt. The new tax plan is causing problems for everyone. And probably the traffic is backed up.

Across the table Mrs. Pell spoons the last of her sherbet into her mouth. Her appetite is returning. Four weeks since the sister died. The sister who was also her roommate. A double loss. His roommate's seat is empty, as always. On what does he exist, Blaustein wonders? Perhaps Ms. Campos puts something aside for him. The son brings candies, seasonal fruit, but how often is that? Once in a blue moon.

Lazar sleeps through his life. Sometime in the morning he will rise, bathe, swallow his medications and lie down again, now on top rather than under the ridged navy blue spread. If Blaustein should catch him then, pleasantries are exchanged. From these moments Blaustein has deduced that Lazar is a person with whom one might pursue a complex line of thought, but alas, Lazar has lost interest. In the Armageddon going on in the outside world. In the meds that might induce him to more activity. Even in his family, their photos stacked haphazardly on his bureau.

Cautiously Blaustein rises from the lunch table. Wends his way through the room exchanging nods, a few humorous words. Always Ceil finished first—she ate daintily, like a bird—and she would be waiting at the water fountain in the corridor. Passing through the door his eyes shift involuntarily to the water fountain. No one is there. Again the pain floods, pins him to the wall. Someone is shouting. Is it he? No, a confused woman pushes against the tide streaming from the dining room. Slowly he straightens. It would be interesting to speak with Lazar sometime about Meryl. No, he means Ceil. Odd that Meryl has not come. Did something go wrong the last time? Occasionally Blaustein gets the sense that something has slipped off the track. It is vague, hard to catch hold of.

* * *

Lunchtime: Meryl shares the park bench with two twenty-somethings. How do they manage all day in those heels? Oily stains from her pizza spread over the surface of the brown bag.

She dawdles, drawing the last drops of the Diet Coke with a long straw. On a patch of grass still summer green, a heron eyes the log where pond turtles arch their crumpled necks into the sun.

The daily drama of pond life rarely fails to absorb her but today Meryl's mind drifts back in time; the candy dish with a petal top that sat forever on the coffee table; the thrum of tires as the family Studebaker sped toward home. Maybe if there were a brother or sister it would be easier. There is no one to share the memories.

One of the twenty-somethings is describing in detail a family drama involving her mother and some cousin or other. Eyes clamped, Meryl strains to conjure up an image of her own mother's face. How can it be that she will never see it again? Despite all the weeks of anticipating the end, Meryl cannot nudge her mind past the one word, 'never.'

She roots through her bag for a tissue, pulls one from the mini-pack along with her blush-on compact, opens it—click— and a skinny six-year-old stares up from gray pile carpeting as her mother slants her face toward the dainty compact in her hand. This is not the everyday lines-tight-around-the-mouth mother but an elegant one, like a queen, with dark waves framing her forehead, wearing a dressing gown with layers of blue chiffon that Meryl can hardly wait to slip on when the babysitter is on the phone.

Now the familiar compact offers Meryl's own forehead, her blotched cheeks. In the sunlight, laugh lines morph into garden-variety wrinkles. And when was the last time she primped for an evening out? She can't recall. These days her work life often leaks into the evening.

Lately the tax partner worms his widowed brother into every conversation. Just a drink, he insists. A friendly meeting of two professionals. No need to commit to an evening. But even that would require small talk and serious attention to her make-up. She hasn't worn her contacts in months.

One decent night's sleep would be a blessing. Night after night she thrashes, her body aching with the essential need to connect, to cling on.

A core intelligence is flooding Meryl's mind: a grieving old man wants only to feel her womanness, to blunt the loss, retard his passage down the corridor, and what possible harm can it cause if he presses her breasts, grazes her mouth with his tongue? This is not rape. This is need, pure and simple. The most basic: to touch life, to connect.

* * *

Blaustein's tired feet carry him onward toward his afternoon nap. Past the door half open where Mrs. Pell dabs at her eyes. Briefly her aroma trails him. Past Ms. Campos, whose head rests more loosely now on her neck muscles. The social worker has asked him to stop by later in the day. What can that be about?

* * *

The next day and shortly after three o'clock Meryl slips out of the office. Despite the crises pressing from all sides. She visualizes Ben, a tiny, round caricature, perched in his customary chair, staring hopefully down the hall.

The highway is open yet Meryl crawls, exasperating the SUV in back, which passes her with a flash of a finger. She's exaggerated the whole business. It will be fine. Ben will question her with sharp interest: the girls' grades, the goings-on at the firm. They will cluck over the petty politicking. Then he will catch her up on his news: the Residents' Council, the newest drama on the Unit.

"Here every day is a soap opera, a telenovela," he will sum up.

As the EZ Pass arm lifts: And if it happens again she will be firm. Re-direct his hand, turn her face away. It's Ben, for goodness sake, dear sensible Ben.

Scant sunlight reflects off the bridge towers as she turns into a parking space. The timing is perfect. Ben will be returning any minute from Chorus. If she stands directly in front of the nursing station he will spot her as he makes the turn into the corridor. He will squint, hand to his forehead against the glare. He will urge his feet faster, faster.

She reaches back into the car, pulls her jacket from the front seat just in case. Damn, she forgot the fruit: prunes, apricots, cranberries culled from the grocer's bins on her way home from the office on Monday night. The manager waited impatiently, one hand on the metal outer grid already lowered halfway. She was the last customer.

Stepping from the elevator, Meryl hides her awkwardness beneath a broad smile. Behind the console Ms. Campos's eyes widen. She smiles back thinly, embarrassed perhaps by the phone conversation.

Mr. Blaustein has not yet come back from Chorus. He should be here at any moment. She has spoken to the social worker and also the Unit doctor. She is not permitted to discuss the meds but the situation seems to be under control. Recently there are signs he is turning a corner.

And here he is, at the end of the corridor, his head tilted in toward Mrs. Pell at his side. One foot after the other, Blaustein and Mrs. Pell inch toward them. She is saying something and he is listening with full attention, his eyeglasses slipping downward. A small joke perhaps because now he is chuckling. Mrs. Pell tips her head to look into his face. With one finger she pushes his glasses up on the bridge of his nose.

"Oh God." Meryl covers her mouth with her hand. "I mean..." She flashes a wild look at the slowly advancing pair, clutches her handbag to her chest. "It's only eight weeks..." The corridor, the console, the handrails along the wall weave in and out of familiarity. "But how...?"

"Come." Ms. Campos takes her arm. "Here, around the corner." Steers her past a medicine cart to an alcove where Meryl drops into a padded chair.

"I had no idea. Did my mother...?" Her eyes fill. Ms. Campos holds out a tissue. Meryl ignores it. With a balled-up fist, she blots at her cheeks. "I mean, does his daughter know? How long...?"

"No, no," Ms. Campos interrupts. "Just yesterday. I noticed it first after breakfast." She snaps her fingers. "Just like that. He loved your mother very much. Everyone remarked. It happens sometimes with the elderly. The daughter too is surprised. She asked after you."

A quiet moment. Ms. Campos picks at her arm patch; a cell phone chirps. Meryl sits stock still, her attention fixed now on a trickle of coffee stains on the carpet. A clutch of nurses has gathered at the console where angry words spew from the small TV tucked into an inner shelf. "*Imbecil, hijo de puta.*" The nurses crowd in, transfixed.

Slowly Meryl straightens, skims a tentative hand over her skirt.

Ms. Campos stands too. "Life is full of surprises. Well I know." She reaches her hand out. "Come. There is a small staff room. A cup of tea would be good."

"No." Meryl shakes her head, blinks. Her eyes fill. "I need to go." A wave of nausea threatens. With effort, she breathes largely into her chest, then, reaching into her bag, fumbles for the car keys.

"Ah. But you must sit for a moment. In the staff room, I think. That would be good."

"No." Bringing all her concentration to bear, Meryl pokes fiercely in the bag. "Damn," she mutters.

Violins rise to a climax from the small TV as the segment ends. The nurses groan, elbow one another companionably, disperse onto the Unit.

"Okay, here they are." Meryl pulls out the car keys.

Ms. Campos shrugs. "If you insist." She holds out the jacket for Meryl to slip her arms into. "The car is in the Visitors Lot?"

Meryl nods.

"The jacket. You should button it. The wind plays tricks this time of year."

* * *

Clicking open the car door, Meryl adjusts herself behind the wheel, sets her bag on the seat alongside, carefully calibrates the tilt of the seatback, the lumbar support, the rear and sideview mirrors—there is Ms. Campos halfway up the path, dragging on a cigarette. Again the nausea threatens. Again she inhales, clenches—one, two—slowly exhales. She bends foward, inserts the key into the ignition. Then she sits for a long, long time staring ahead as, through the thinning light, tiny cars move inexorably across the broad expanse of bridge and the darkness spreads.

SOUPGREENS

WHEN IT CAME TIME FOR Tanya to die, I walked up to Broadway and 98th in the morning to Harry the butcher and ordered a fresh spring chicken, cut into eighths. Harry said he hadn't seen me for a while. Fact is, I no longer cooked, beyond heating up the occasional take-out with Gil in his condo. I hadn't prepared a proper meal in—it was hard to remember when. Cordially, I remarked to Harry how well he was looking. Harry returned the compliment and sent his best regards home. At the Korean market on the corner I picked up a bunch of fresh dill, celery, carrots and an onion.

When I got back Tanya was lying, face flattened onto her paws, on the pink chenille bath mat Martin and I had lain for her ten days before, over an old plastic mackinaw in my workroom, between the desk chair and the corner bookcase. We had stopped walking her. Despite everyone's best efforts, her emissions were no longer controllable. Before I stopped minding, I had actually fashioned a diaper for her, with a hole for her mangy, wet-look tail. Soon after, she had given up her wanderings through the apartment. Small comfort.

I brought the pot to a simmer and added the chicken, carrots, celery and the onion. When I passed the workroom Tanya had raised her nose—the fibrous tendons in her neck strained almost to the breaking point—and held it for several seconds, sniffing the air. It was impossible to misread the pleasure in her profoundly dear, ugly face. The appointment at the vet's was not until five-thirty. Martin had promised to be home twenty minutes before. Together we would carry her over.

Sheer cowardice had kept me under the blankets overtime that morning. From the kitchen, WINS all-news all-the-time riveted down the hall. Martin's morning fix. I was working up the strength to holler for him to lower it for Christ sake, when abruptly the noise stopped. Martin walked into the bedroom with his coffee and sat down on the window seat facing me.

I looked up, my eyes raw. "Where is she?"

Martin gestured toward the workroom, "I filled up her water bowl," and crossed a tidy leg. "Em, it's time." His voice was rehearsed and matter-of-fact. "No need for recriminations. I've spoken to a lawyer. I'll be out of here by the first of the week."

"Are you out of your mind?" My voice bolted to its topmost pitch. "Today? I can't think about that today."

"Calm down. There's nothing to think about. I'm letting you know. Put it out of your mind until tomorrow if it's too much for today."

"Who did you speak to?" I shot at him. "Lisa? Fucking Mona Lisa, the lawyer-lover? How convenient for you. Did you tell her we were putting our dog to sleep today? Did you tell her that?" My eyes spilled over.

"Goddam, I'm sick to death of always being wrong." He stood up, slanted his head toward my dressing table mirror, fiddled with his tie. "I'm in meetings most of the day but I'll be back in time for Tanya."

Involuntarily my head swiveled to the door, half expecting to see her scuttle in, tail tucked under, and belly under the bed, which is where she had fled for the past eighteen years whenever voices were raised for any reason whatsoever. Where she had fled fourteen months earlier when I made a similar announcement and the year before that when Martin had and—. You get the picture. But she was beyond that now. I left a message with the concierge in London for Gil to call me the moment he checked in. Then I crawled into shabby jeans, walked up to Harry's, read through some Czerny lying on the piano, backed up my hard drive.

Real work was out of the question. On a dozen pretexts I found myself drawn into the workroom. Once I bent, took her face in my hands and kissed the tender spot at the peak of her head, then rubbed my cheek back and forth against it. Tanya growled gently. Her great liquid eyes, once her prize feature, were milky with age.

After an hour I ground a turn of fresh pepper into the broth, added the dill, poked at the chicken with a long fork. Another twenty minutes, I estimated. The apartment was powerfully fragrant. I imagined young children riding in the elevator past our floor and inhaling deeply, jealously. Pure fantasy, I knew. The sublime aroma had no resonance for contemporary kids. In truth, it would have none for our own kids. Ah, well. It was for my solace then, and Tanya's. I inhaled gratefully.

At noontime I telephoned my lawyer. "Can you believe it? Martin informed me this morning that he's moving out next week. The morning of the day we're putting Tanya down. He has it all set up with Lisa. Can you believe it?"

"I'm a matrimonial lawyer, Em. There's nothing on the face of the earth I can't believe."

I loved her cynicism, which extended globally to every aspect of life.

"No problem," she went on. "We're prepared. Do you want me to contact Lisa?"

"Oh God, not today." I ran a hand through my growing-out perm. "I need some breathing space between life crises."

"Then I'll wait to hear from you. Tell me, what do you think the percentages are it'll happen this time?"

"I don't know. I can't think. My mind aches when I try."

Her tone eased. "Crummy question. Sorry. How's Gil?"

"On his way to London. Bad timing. I left a message for him to phone me as soon as he gets in."

"Do the kids know?"

"About which event?" Not that either will be a surprise, it occurred to me.

"Actually I meant Tanya."

"They're aware that something's up. I didn't want them to feel awful in advance. It's hard when you're so far away. I'll call tonight." I added softly, "After it's over."

"You take it easy, kiddo. I'll be around through the weekend."

The weekend. Would Martin and I drive down to the shore together on Friday to bury Tanya, as planned? After endless back and forth we had arrived at cremation. Given my deepest, unvoiced druthers, she would have been taxidermed and placed permanently on the mat behind my desk chair. I had never actually articulated this notion. How could I, after Martin's terse "Dead is dead?" But finally it had come together. Today was Wednesday.

The vet's office would handle the cremation and return the ashes on Friday morning. We would drive down to Beach Haven, bury the 'delicately painted box of the finest metal' next to Jack the Donkey's tombstone, which had come with the property, decades ago. Apparently the previous owners had been poorly regarded. "Jack wasn't the only jackass lived here then" was a local gag line.

Months before, when the end was still only a wrinkle, long before cremation entered the dialogue, I had spent the bleak first half of a concert pondering the logistics. The subscription seat beside me yawned vacant. Martin was running late or something. That Tanya would be interred at the shore was a given. The best plan was for her to die on a Friday. Then we could pack her right into the car and head south. But that was a long shot. What if she died early in the week, on a Monday or Tuesday? (Here Martin had slipped in, mouthed an apology.) She would need to be refrigerated until the weekend. She was a smallish dog. Maybe, if I emptied out all but the essentials, we could squeeze her into the fridge. Would she fit in the freezer, I'd wondered? A rush of guilty bile rose to my throat. I forced my mind to a blank page.

* * *

The aroma dominated the rooms. Like my grandmother's on a Friday morning. She would pick out her soupgreens, tied with a rubberband, at ancient Gina Masiero's, on the corner.

"Anything else for you, Mrs. Rusoff?"

"Not that I can think of. If I forgot something I'll send down Em, Ruthie's oldest. Only six but already some piano player. A real talent." Grandma could never have understood about Tanya. About the pure and uncomplicated love for a good dog. Domestic animals were irrelevant to the roiling energies of East Third Street. She would never, ever have understood about Lisa. Mona Lisa Hirshhorn, Esquire, Martin's lover for the past six years. Or mine, Gil Beers, whose business required that he spend extended bulks of time abroad. Which suited me, actually. Suited us both.

"Honest to God, Grandma, it's all worked out. Martin and I have the best bad marriage in town."

* * *

I ate lunch at the stove, standing up; bowtie noodles boiled limp, tossed with butter and enough brown sugar to sink a ship. The linoleum surrounding the stove crunched amiably under my feet. From the open shelves over the sink the bag of Iams spewed forth malevolent vibes. Thick sudden rage wrenched my gut. Fucking Martin. I snapped the bag by the neck, gave it a sharp twist and yanked it into the garbage.

At the first visit after Tanya had definitively sworn off her dog food, Doctor Lorne recommended we try Iams, hot from the chemist's lab, nutritionally balanced for the mature canine. And of course it went without saying, he said, no more table scraps. Which translated to no more ziti, bagels and lox, buttermilk pancakes, omelettes au fines herbes. Except for lettuce, Tanya ate everything. No more chicken, her best beloved, her soul food. How many times had Martin or I or the kids catapulted from our beds in the dead of night to be sure that the frail, lethal bones, the prime delicacy, had been removed from the kitchen garbage and thrown into the incinerator. The Iams were an expensive bust. Tanya sniffed them dubiously and outmaneuvered us to the leftover lasagna in the garbage.

Time passed, somehow. Outside, the yellowing leaves caught the October sun. Tanya lay on her mat, tranquil, barely stirring. An occasional thin spasm shook her. Tilted back in my desk chair my mind wandered past the clutter on my desk. I considered the pros and cons of fruitarianism, living on a houseboat, trekking the Andes. Life without Martin. Mona Lisa must be giving him some tough time. What else could explain his atrocious timing this morning? Was she pregnant? Nah. The woman hadn't an eyedrop of estrogen in her. She'd never had an honest-to-God period in her life, I bet.

Shortly after four I showered, shampooed my hair, pulled on my dog-walking sweats. In the kitchen the chicken had cooled down. I worked with my bare hands at the butcher block table. The meat separated easily from the bones. When Martin's keys jangled I was just finishing up.

"Be with you in a minute," he called, heading down the hall as if this were all standard procedure. Another evening with Martin and Em and Tanya, their mature canine. I heaped the chicken into Tanya's bowl and carried it to the workroom. Tanya scrambled onto all fours like a puppy. Tensile. Energized.

"Okay precious doggie girl, here you go."

When Martin emerged in his dog-walking sweater and chinos, Tanya was pigging out, scarfing it down. Ears alert, tail high, extremely busy at her favorite job in the world. He bent to retrieve an errant strand of white meat from the floor, then hung scowling in the doorway.

"Relax," I said. "It's okay. It'll make her sick as hell when it hits her digestive tract, I know, but that'll take a good thirty minutes. She'll be gone by then."

He raised an eyebrow, refilled the water bowl. Joyfully Tanya lapped at it. Her hindquarters wriggled with delight.

BLAUSTEIN'S KISS

We wrapped her in a navy blue Martex bathtowel. Her head poked free in the elevator and hung over Martin's arm like a gargoyle.

"That was a nice thing you did," he said to me.

"Yeah, I think so. The apartment smelled heavenly all day. Reminded me of my Grandma's."

"She was a good lady."

"The best." My eyes filled. Predictably, Martin looked elsewhere.

"You should have taken a sweater," he said. "I mean, it's October."

Tanya growled contentedly in his arms. Being cradled in a soft towel with a full, happy stomach was dog paradise. I strode alongside, occasionally scratching the sticking-out top of her head. At the dairy restaurant on the corner, the proprietor stood in the doorway, catching the late-day sun. "Tanya under the weather?" he called. We moved at a brisk pace through the streaming sidewalks.

* * *

"I'll give you a minute alone," said Dr. Lorne. Tanya lay on the examining table, spent, enervated. We were all coming down from the poultry high. At the door she had edged nervously in the towel and twitched her paws, a sad imitation of her usual hyperbolic performance at the vet's. I kissed again that spot at the tip of her head, Martin patted her pitiful flank. Her great liquid eyes were mildly interested. Doctor Lorne slipped back into the cubicle.

"The best doggie the best doggie the best doggie," I crooned. Her eyes closed, shut out the light. She breathed deeply one time, I felt my face break apart as the spirit oozed from her, moved sobbing, sobbing to Martin, who was sobbing too. We clung to one another.

[106]

"She's gone," the vet said.

The occupants of the waiting room drew their pets closer as we stumbled in and stared kindly in other directions. Martin handed me the folded bath towel and turned to the paperwork at the desk. I slumped onto a soft chair, cradled my head in the towel. Then we were done. The late bright sunlight stung, an affront, as we lurched through the front door. Blindly I turned from it and headed east, away from the sun, toward nowhere. Martin followed behind.

We had gone several blocks before Martin's peremptory hand on my elbow slowed me to a halt.

"Em, I'll tell you what. I just need to make a phone call. Change some plans. Then we could walk home together. Spend a quiet evening, maybe talk things over."

We crossed a broad avenue and wove onto a street of brownstones and bare-limbed trees, and then another. Reflective, subdued.

"Well," I said, and leaned against a hydrant. The gray dusk streamed over me like a blessing. "Actually, you should go on with your plan."

Martin's graying eyebrows rose toward his hairline.

"I'll walk awhile before heading home," I said. "The fresh air feels good. Do you mind taking the towel?"

"So then." He tucked it under an arm, turned away and back again. "Watch yourself, Em. You're more upset than you realize."

Across from us a tattered old woman steadied herself on a gingko.

"Maybe," I said. "Thanks."

She reached into a pocket, flung out a fat handful of crumbs. As if on cue a swarm of street birds burst from the air, pecking gratefully. Martin looked full into my face, turned, crossed the street at the corner. My eyes followed until the final speck of him dissolved into the grayness, then I turned too and walked on, under the lifting sky, into the warm, enormous night.

LOVESICKNESS

"HE HOLDS ME AGAINST the wall and rams it in," was how Sheila put it.

"But what about your parents? Where are they?"

"They left already. I told you that a hundred times." She leans exasperated weight into one hip. "They leave early for work."

I tap two Chiclets from the shiny box, pass it on to Audrey, and bite in past the shell to the gummy sweetness.

"Tell it again. The part before he sticks it in."

"Again?" Sheila rolls her no-color eyes heavenward. "Oh, okay."

An atom bomb could explode in that coatroom and we three girls would not budge from our huddle.

"I'm completely dressed except for my coat and my panties which I stuck in the coat pocket beforehand. I'm checking my geometry problems and the buzzer rings. Ten after eight on the dot. I open up the door to listen and when I'm sure it's him coming up the stairs I pull the barrette out of my hair so it falls partway over my forehead and go lean against the far wall. He likes for me to be the first thing he sees when he enters the room."

In my mind he's scaling the steps four at a time. "And then?"

"He sticks his briefcase on the table next to my looseleaf and pulls it out. Meantime I'm hitching up my skirt. Then he walks over, holds me against the wall and rams it in."

"All the way?"

"Of course all the way. And it's really big. And quivering."

"Quivering?"

I stop chewing to better comprehend that information. "I didn't know they quivered."

"Some do. There are all different kinds."

We are alone in the universe. Jackets are flying over hooks, shriek, shove, giggle, Kilroy was where? We are alone in the universe.

Audrey's assembly blouse is stuck to her armpits. "But what if you get pregnant? Your life could be ruined forever."

"For Chrissake, it's not like we're babies. He takes care of that. He says not to waste my time thinking about it. That's his department." No, she shakes her head to Audrey's offer of the Chiclets.

"Exactly how does it feel," Audrey asks, "When he rams it in?"

Sheila's eyes roll skyward again.

I am trying to imagine how it could possibly not hurt a lot. Also, I'm trying to figure out where Sheila's feet are.

Audrey persists. "Even the first time? How did it feel the first time? I bet it hurt like hell."

A pause, then quietly: "It was worth it."

The early morning coatroom smells of steam heat and salami wrapped in waxed paper.

"And then?"

"Then he pulls it out and stuffs it back into his pants, dope. What do you think?"

Audrey wants to know if he wipes it off or anything.

"I told you. There's no time. He has to catch the 8:30 bus. If he's late the boss gives him hell."

I'm wondering how to ask if he ever says anything, like I love you.

"Does he talk about his family? His wife or his kids?"

"This has nothing to do with them. This is between us." Her tone is holy.

"So he just turns around and walks out?"

Sheila considers. "Well, sometimes he looks in the bathroom mirror to be sure his tie is hanging right."

"And what are you doing then?"

"Thinking."

"Thinking?"

"Thinking how the hours will creep on and on until the next morning finally arrives. Missing him in advance."

"Oh."

We are silent out of respect for Sheila's burden of lovesickness. The radiator clangs. Someone sneezes. Down the block a church bell sounds. And through the unwashed windows light slants into the schoolroom, where the day will pass slowly.

THE FUGITIVE

THE QUILT IN THE back seat squirms. I veer precipitously through the toll plaza from EZ PASS ONLY into ALL OTHER SERVICES, cutting off a cabbie who rams savage weight onto his horn. My attention is glued to the rear view mirror. Definitely a lump is breathing under that quilt. Larger than a cat. A muffled two-tone cough escapes.

It's impossible that only minutes have passed since I drove out through the nursing home gates. Brooding about Dad, who seems more absent every week. And Michael. Still sulking. Still trying to push this better-than-most part-time relationship into something more. Even though I told him up front, at the beginning, that I would never again live full-time with anyone, ever.

A long "shh" unwinds from the back seat, then a thin shred of voice. "It's all right. I'm a pacifist. Please don't turn me in." And to my astonishment I obey. Slip into automatic bridge toll mode, hand out the change, sing "Have a good day" to the toll collector. Several yards later I screech the Volvo onto the right shoulder of the highway and click off the ignition. A plaid shirt shoulder pokes from the mound of quilt, then a sleeve, and finally the rest of a decrepit and very old man, bowtie askew, fingers fastened onto a worn plastic bag.

"How do you do? My name is Jacob Perlow."

An awareness clicks in: I have seen this threadworn shirt and the wrinkled face over it, more than once, somewhere.

"What are you doing in my car?" I am beyond the ability to control my voice.

"There was no other way. Believe me, I've wracked my brain."

A Jeep Cherokee slows down beside us. I wave it away. "What are you talking about?"

"My escape," he says. "I would have much preferred not involving you but that proved impossible. So often in the past week I have wished that I could discuss the situation with your father but alas, that is no longer an option." He gestures, palms skyward. I have placed him now, the scholarly slow-moving one three doors down from Dad, who returns my greeting each week with a courtly nod of the head.

Around us the traffic swarms southward.

"It was not all bad." Jacob pauses to adjust the hearing aid planted in his left ear. "Especially the first few years, the cuisine more than adequate, companionship, cultural activities, not to mention the Wellness Center. What more could one ask for?" He has eased into an oratorical mode. "In time a few pesky health problems surfaced but that would have happened anywhere. Then overnight it all changed."

Jacob's face looms in the rearview mirror. "A new roommate, a Cossack, the roommate from Hell. Imagine, while I am davenning the morning prayers he reads aloud from magazines of a lurid nature." Jacob blots at his forehead with a soiled handkerchief. "He disappears for hours into our shared lavatory, unresponsive to my knocks and pleadings. Night after night he dials the telephone to numbers answered always by young ladies who specialize in describing the most intimate experiences. And how do I know this?" Pause. "Because he pushes in the speaker button on the phone so that I cannot help but hear every word."

Outside the window, gulls swoop and glide. The river is wrapped in a thin gray haze. I have shifted sideways into the passenger seat, my attention fully focused on the wretched old man in back.

"A chemical imbalance, an illness perhaps, but these days sympathy is not uppermost in my mind."

Elliott, his son, intervened strenuously but to no avail. He, Jacob, met with Elliott and the social worker, who explained that it was in their best interests, trust her, if roommates ironed out difficulties of this nature between themselves. A private room, he pleaded? You know the rule, Mr. Perlow, she said firmly. No private rooms. In a situation of this peculiarity, surely an exception could be made. No exceptions. Finally he had carried the problem to the Internal Activities Panel, not without first advising the other party, who spat into a used Kleenex and turned his back.

Jacob sighs, "Who can argue with testosterone?"

The hearing went poorly, antagonisms running amok. Here Jacob's distress spills over.

"Oh, poor thing." I yank open the glove compartment, grab a fistful of tissues from a wrinkled mini-pack.

Jacob blots at his eyes. "Simple sleep deprivation," he murmurs. "No cause for concern." Laboriously he cranks down the window, inhales. So now Elliott has gone to Stanford on sabbatical leave and although they speak every Sunday it is clear that the move has created a certain psychological distance as well. The social worker has turned her attention to problems more appropriate to her intervention, and then three weeks ago—Abruptly the narrative stops.

"This is indelicate. It is not something one repeats to a woman."

"Jacob. Please. Times have changed. There are new rules."

"I am aware." He turns his face to the side. It was heartbreaking. Mrs. Gersh, a new resident, not six weeks a widow, poor thing, obviously still adrift in a sea of grief and confusion, enticed to the roommate's bed in the dead of night. A crude thumb in Jacob's direction: "Him? Even when he's awake he's unconscious." First caresses, then demands and finally wrenching sobs. "But I can't bend that way anymore." After that Jacob began planning.

I swallow hard, "Poor Mrs. Gersh," and return him to the larger point. "But why my car? And when did you slip in?"

Jacob consults a pocket watch safety-pinned to his pants pocket.

"About two hours ago. I was waiting outside the garage, near the laundry." A thread of pride creeps into his voice. "I've been surveilling for weeks. I know that you visit always on Tuesday mornings. Also that your back door on the driver's side is never locked. The quilt on the back seat was the deciding factor." It lies in a rumpled heap on the floor. "Actually I had it narrowed down to two of you. Perhaps you know Mr. Mueller?"

"Maybe if I saw him."

"Trust me, you would enjoy meeting his daughter. A charming individual. But her car is only a two-door model. You may perhaps have noted some slight impairment in my mobility?"

I taste a certain sourness in my mouth.

Leaning forward Jacob pats the shoulder of my windbreaker. "Even if she drove a four-door I would have chosen you. I'm certain."

* * *

[116]

Jacob stares high into the ceiling of the lobby. "This is some grand adventure." We are working our way through the gaping expanse of marble under the doorman's mesmerized eye. He stops mid-span. "I must repeat, this was not part of my plan. You were to deposit me on a street corner, after which a taxi would carry me to a hotel. I have unduly inconvenienced you."

"Jacob, please. You need to move along. We'll talk upstairs." Already there has been mention of an impending call of nature. The priority is to get into the apartment. Put together some lunch. Then we can figure out the next move. Hadn't my father always warned against making decisions on an empty stomach?

Two days later. The situation in the apartment is stable, Jacob proclaims. God knows what's happening at the Home. The first evening Jacob phoned in from the pay phone on the corner—to counter attempts at tracing the call, he explained. They were not to worry. He'd be back in touch. I would have given a month's salary to be a fly on the wall of the nurses' station. Outside the phone booth, the first moist hint of Indian summer swept Michael back into my mind. It had been five days. We'd never been out of touch that long before. Had he bought that giant treadmill he was looking at? We needed to talk. About Jacob. About lots of things. I bet his allergies were acting up. They always did, this time of year.

Information is exchanged. I know by rote the unending virtues of Esther, Jacob's late wife, and the shattering pain of her loss—thank God it was sudden, Esther never knew a thing, but difficult for Jacob, for whom some preparation might have eased the shock. The joys and tribulations of his thirty-three years in charge of the books at Manor Furs. Esther also worked there part-time, filing.

His daughter Tamar on the West Bank with her husband. A constant anxiety. And Elliott, the PhD. The philosopher. But to be perfectly frank, a thinker not a doer. More like him, Jacob, in that respect than his mother, rest in peace.

Jacob knows all about the horrific divorce; my daughter, Sarah, in Spokane; Rosie, my granddaughter, who is nearly six; my absurdly underpaid job at the Arts Institute; Dad's research; the medal received at the White House; the dementia. I have not yet mentioned Michael.

My mind is busy catastrophizing. I need a handrail in the shower. For the couple of days he'll be here? How long are we talking about anyway? Why doesn't he call his son? Should I take the initiative? But that would undermine his feelings of autonomy. And what about medications? Jacob insists that only two are critical, the cardiac ones, and he has a week's supply of each in his shopping bag, along with several changes of underwear, socks, a fresh shirt, pajamas, a toothbrush, some snapshots folded into a frayed address book and his tallis and t'fillin.

"And after they run out?"

"I must demur, Lucy." He waggles an index finger. "One day at a time, we agreed."

Jacob sleeps like an infant at night, in the bedroom, over his strenuous objections. "No, no. I cannot further discommode you."

"Just tonight, Jacob. Indulge me. Just tonight," while I field phone calls from the sofa bed in the living room. Neighbors whom I've barely met check in.

Sarah phones. "I'm receiving some weird vibes here, Mom. Everything okay?"

I return the call when I know she will be out.

"What a shock," I tell the voice mail. "One moment I'm driving down the highway feeling teary about Grandpa, when suddenly—" I sum up, "I know it's crazy but how could I take him back? I mean, he's a lovely guy."

At night my body roots through the blankets for Michael while Dad, a young Dad, wiry, opinionated, drifts in and out of my dreams. With the first light Jacob's morning prayers invade my consciousness and I wonder for the hundredth time what this old man is doing in my life.

Some things I decide not to tell: that his incessant coughing is driving me crazy, as is his habit of dicing his food into tiny cubes and his need to report the smallest incident in lavish detail. That the arithmetic does not add up: he is older than the ninety years he admits to.

Jacob too keeps secrets, I learn afterward. That a salt shaker on the table is more thrilling than sex. That he has stopped praying to die. That he was aware of my phone call to Michael late last night.

The third morning. I push up the sleeves of Michael's workshirt, duck my nose into its collar for a quick fix of his morning smell.

Across the table, Jacob pushes his cereal bowl to the side. After breakfast he'll stroll up to the newsstand and pick up the Forward. Sunlight streams in through the kitchen window as Jacob checks out a banana, which he likes "flecked with brown."

Now I set down the Times. "Jacob, I'm concerned. About Elliott." Jacob nods. "So am I."

I continue. "Specifically, by now he must know that you're missing—"

Jacob is piling the used plates. "Perhaps."

"Definitely. The Home will have contacted him. It's their obligation."

"But no mention in the press, as I predicted. They can't allow word of an escape to circulate." He starts to rise.

"Probably true. But Elliott is different. There are legalities to consider. I'm sure that in cases like this the family is notified."

Verticality is achieved. "Ah, but to the best of my knowledge, Lucy, there has never been a successful escape from Riverdale Park. Remember, I lived there for eight years. I'm the first. Numero Uno. A few hysterical incidents perhaps." All effort is galvanized now toward forward movement. "Suitcases packed, taxis called in the night, but they were easily thwarted."

"Whatever. My point is, Elliott needs to hear from your own lips that you are well, and the sooner the better. Today, in fact." My fingertips thrum the table top. "After that we can plan the next steps."

He shambles in stubborn silence toward the kitchen, plates in hand. Delicately they clink one against the other.

"Oh, and Jacob, don't forget that I'm going into the office for a couple of hours. You have the key?" A twinge irritates my mind. "Listen, no disappearing acts while I'm gone."

Triumph, he has reached the dishwasher. "Lucy, have you lost your senses? Who would flee from Paradise?"

* * *

Quickly I fumble my key into the lock. There he is, thank goodness, asleep on the couch, covered belt downward with the piano shawl, shoes lined up obediently on the needlepoint rug. His waist widens, then shrinks, with each reassuring breath. An elongated hiss releases from his mouth. I slant backward to ease the door shut, slide the grocery bags onto the counter. A sheet of toweling is Scotch-taped to the microwave: *12:30 P.M. The phone rang twice. We are running low on skim milk. Also Kleenex. Perhaps tonight you will permit me to take you to dinner.*

He has used my absence to remove himself from the bedroom, which looks tidier than it has in years, the wastebasket emptied, the clutter of books on the nightstand aligned.

The answering machine is blinking twice.

"Luce, is this Jacob guy gonna be there at dinner? I mean, what's the story?"

And: "A stranger? You brought a total stranger into your home? Mom, for God's sake. Call me back."

Rustlings from the living room. "Lucy, is that you?"

Quickly I rummage in my top drawer for the snapshot of Michael, banished in the fevered moments after the fight, replace it onto the nightstand. "So Jacob, you've been busy, I see."

"Merely rectifying an error. I have moved my belongings to the floor of the hall closet but if you would prefer—"

"Jacob, please." I gesture broadly from the living room door.

"Who needs palaces?" He struggles toward a sitting-up posture. "You will be amazed by my adventures this morning."

"Adventures?" I perch on the edge of the wing chair across from him. Ten minutes, I admonish myself.

"I intended merely to glance in at the dairy restaurant down the block. Serendipity. Not only was there an instant rapport with Mendel, the owner, but his niece may have worked in the office with Esther. He will investigate and let me know." His feet hang downward, like a child's. "Then on the way back I stopped to chat with the doorman, Jose—a fine fellow, largely self-educated—and guess what?" No response is required. "He has offered to tutor me in Spanish. He will draw up a syllabus over the weekend. Believe me, by the time I got back I was ready for a nap."

"I can imagine."

"A red-letter morning."

"And Elliott?" I ask.

"Ahhh. I knew I forgot something." He smacks the side of his head. "It slipped my mind. That happens to me sometimes, perhaps you have noticed? But now about dinner. We can order in as usual but I hope you will accept my invita—"

"Actually I've invited a guest."

"Oh?"

"A friend. A close friend."

Jacob's eyes widen.

"Michael Byrne. He's an oboist. The Aspen Winds? You'll like him, I think."

"No question about it," Jacob says firmly. "His name alone evokes respect, 'Mich-a-el, who is like God.' So now." He grips the sofa arm, rocks backward for momentum, hoists onto his feet. "We must roll up our sleeves. You can count on me to handle the bar and—"

"That's Michael's territory," I cut in. "Bloody Marys especially."

"Ah, Bloody Marys." Jacob busies himself in the folding of the piano shawl, the fringe overflowing his arms.

"Also there's some white wine open and a bottle of Madeira somewhere."

"Madeira. Esther and I spent a memorable day there. On a cruise out of Portugal. She—"

"We did too. Last year. The Aspens did a gig on the ship."

"Gig?" He and the fringe are enmeshed in mortal combat.

"Job. You know, concerts."

"Of course," says Jacob. "Makes perfect sense."

I reach out a hand for the shawl.

* * *

Michael's gray crewcut is tight against his skull, his face lightly summer-toasted. A fleck of white shaving cream clings to the patch of skin closest to his left ear. His shirt is tucked decorously into his jeans for the occasion. There's even a silver-buckled belt. I fold into his chest and feel down to my toes the blood-rush of him.

A door opens and Jacob shuffles from the bathroom, shoes shined to a high polish, bowtie perked at his neck.

"Michael, this is—"

"How do you do, I'm Jacob Perlow. A pleasure to meet you." Jacob plants himself, extends a firm hand. "Please come in. Make yourself comfortable." He gestures toward the sofa where the pillows are plumped into a state of military preparedness.

Michael's eyes carry a certain edge. "Well, hello. Glad to meet you." He returns the handshake warily. "Sorry I'm late. Rehearsal ran over." He turns abruptly, blows his nose into a tissue pulled from his pocket. "Damn allergies."

"Please," Jacob glows. "It is an honor."

Michael sniffs the air, "Can that smell be coming from this kitchen?" He heads for his customary wing chair, shifts. "Before I sit down, can I make some drinks? Jacob?"

The briefest beat. "A Bloody Mary perhaps?"

* * *

The roast chicken aroma permeates the apartment. Blissfully I inhale. Jacob reaches for a thigh. "Personally I'm a dark meat man." And a potato. "Esther also preferred Idahos."

Michael's eyes scan the table top. "Sour cream?"

Fiercely I shake my head and mouth, "Kashruth."

Michael's face is widely uncomprehending.

I drag out the syllables. "Kaaashroouuth."

"Ah. Would you pass the salad?"

Jacob misses the exchange completely. He has been totally occupied since we sat down, margarining every inch of his roll, likewise his baked potato, salting down everything in sight.

Outside, the babble of traffic begins to subside.

"So now, Michael." Jacob brings full attention to bear. "I have many questions. This is the first time I have the pleasure of meeting a distinguished musician."

Michael smiles skeptically.

"Maybe this is a good moment to give Elliott a ring," I interject.

"Ah yes, Elliott. But it will be late after that." Jacob is distressed. "My stamina is no longer what it once was."

Michael nods. "Why not postpone the lecture until breakfast?"

"Breakfast?" I swerve from the dishwasher.

"Yes. In the morning." Jacob dodders a few steps, his face planed into peculiar angles. "So now." With effort he regroups. "May I use the bedroom, Lucy? It should take only a few moments."

I wave the question away.

Swiftly, before the door jamb clicks, Michael envelops me. "Come here, you."

"Hey, wait a second." I wrestle free, stumble backward into the dishwasher.

"Lucy?" Michael's shirt has pulled free in back and lops over his belt.

I'm panting, my hand pressed into the pulse-point at my neck. "He's liable to pop out at any moment. Needs the other glasses. Can't get a dial tone."

Michael backs off. "By the time he gets it together to pop out we could swim around Manhattan Island." His tone is laced with injury.

"And I'm not sure about staying over. You saw his reaction?"

Before my eyes Michael's features tighten, harden, set.

"Just a few more nights." My voice is childish, mollifying.

"What is this? Some prehistoric charmer has taken control of your life. He's even lured you into the kitchen."

I'm immobilized, glued onto one square of kitchen tile.

Michael ranges the living room. "Damn it, Lucy, when Rosie came that time, you asked me not to stay over because it might confuse her, whatever that's supposed to mean. And now this character! Welcome to the millennium, for Christ sake."

The argument rachets down the timeworn track: accusation, recrimination, then a new wrinkle: "Well, I don't know," he says. "Maybe we need to try it alone. I'm not sure about this part-time business anymore...I mean, it's been four years...and if you really can't handle something permanent..."

Suddenly I'm crying hard, hiccuping, and Michael is not drawing me into his arms, offering Kleenex. My hands agitate the pockets of my skirt. No tissues. I blow my nose hard into a sheet of kitchen toweling. "It's that, you know...I mean, since your apartment is stabilized..."

An extended pause. Finally, "Luce, I've tried to be patient, I know where you're coming from. I do, believe me." He sighs, his face lined with exhaustion. "But this is only half a life. Face it, we're not kids."

Awkwardly I mop at my eyes. Long moments pass. "I don't know. Maybe it is time." A tic shudders through my upper body. "I mean, two apartments? Two rents?" And now I hear myself agreeing, begging in fact, for Michael to give up his apartment and move in here with me, which I thought after the divorce I could never again tolerate.

Michael hangs long in the kitchen doorway. "Lucy, do you hear what you're saying?"

* * *

One a.m.: We peep through the bedroom door. Jacob is asleep on the bedspread, curled like an ancient fetus, the phone receiver beside him. Michael and I turn to the living room couch.

Three a.m.: furtive clinks infiltrate from the kitchen. The dishwasher is being loaded.

Six thirty: elaborate honks and coughing from the bathroom.

Six forty: the morning prayers.

"Wha-a-a? What's that?" Michael floats just under the surface.

"Shhhh." I curl an arm around his head, he lops a long thigh over mine, we drift into blessed slumber.

In a faraway land a toilet flushes. The pillow next to mine is empty. When Michael slips back next to me I release again into the sheets. In a moment his breathing will settle into a deep, easy—

"A new guest has arrived," Michael whispers.

"What?"

"It might be that homeless guy who works the number 2 train in the mornings. Or maybe Burl Ives. Did he wear glasses? I can't remember. Don't worry. Your buddy Jacob has it under control." Michael reaches out a long arm, "Come here, Granny."

"Michael. What the—" I push up from his chest. Jacob's voice winds from the kitchen, mixes with another. "Stop kidding around. Who is it?"

"I don't know. Who can keep track of your social life these days?"

"Shit." I fumble for the floor, the t-shirt on the bureau, a flipflop nearby.

Michael waves my underpants from under the nest of sheets. "You never know. It may be black-tie." He falls back into the pillow. "Keep in touch."

The kitchen table is laid with my Guatemalan placemats, the coffee mugs that almost match. I hang like a wraith in the doorway for a long moment before Jacob sees me.

"Ah, Lucy." He pushes upward. "Good morning. Look here, a surprise."

My eyes are riveted onto the new arrival crumpled into a kitchen chair, his shirt blotched with smears of ketchup and grease, his beard a tangle.

"Permit me to introduce my son, Elliott. And this is the angel, Lucy."

Elliott strains to his feet and extends a gummy hand. "How do you do," he begins with energy. "I must thank you for all…" His voice slides downhill into odd diphthongs.

Jacob leaps in. "I apologize for not forewarning you but Elliott has caught me unawares as well. I merely left the message on his machine that—"

"I took the red-eye," Elliott informs a space somewhere over my head. His upper lip grimaces to his nose, positioning his glasses.

"Not an hour ago I returned with the newspaper and there he stood, with Jose. I could barely believe my eyes." He clasps Elliott's shoulder in a fat squeeze-and-release. "So now."

Jacob begins to pour the Tropicana, holding tight to the carton with both hands. An orange stream travels down the outside of one of the glasses. The t-shirt is rough against my naked nipples. SAVE THE WHALES. From the wings, couch springs creak. A window shade snaps. The focus shifts to the living room.

"That's the archangel, Michael," I explain.

* * *

Half an hour has passed. A residue of sleep coats my eyelids. Tenderly I gaze across the table at Michael, the bristle of crumbs that clings to his lower lip. Only Jacob is fully functional. "I can't imagine what came over me last night. One minute I was replacing the telephone receiver and the next…"

Valiantly Elliott struggles to remain awake. His head jerks abruptly upward, droops; his eyes widen, shrink, widen again. A torn Ked agitates the table leg. Experimentally he shapes his lips, blurts finally, "Papa, we must start to plan…" The fragment floats on the air. Jacob regards his son with cool interest. "Despite Lucy's generosity it is not—"

Sharply Jacob cuts in, "There are new rules nowadays, son."

Elliott shrivels into his chest. My eyes widen. Well. Here is a new side of Jacob.

Jacob continues in a milder tone, "It is time for me to move on, I agree."

"Jacob, you are welcome here for as long…"

"Lucy, it is time. Everyone knows about fish and guests. And now Elliott can help me to explore the options."

Elliott's head bobs like a wind-up toy's.

"I have seen in the Yellow Pages that excellent hotel arrangements are available. Perhaps I might find one in the neighborhood."

Mutely I nod. My eyes travel across to Michael, who catches my glance and winks.

"Also, Jose has extended an invitation for me to move in with him and his mother. The younger sisters would double up, freeing a bedroom. Frankly, the family can use the rental income."

A wave of naked jealousy breaks over me. "Where do they live?"

"Not far." He continues, "Another possibility is Mendel at the dairy restaurant, whose niece may well have worked with Esther."

"Momma?" bleats Elliott.

Jacob ignores him. "With the children gone, he and his wife ramble about in a spacious eight-room cooperative. An empty nest. A poetical turn of phrase, don't you agree?" He leans in. "I have reason to believe that they would welcome me into their home. Now that he is contemplating retirement, Mendel is eager to expand his intellectual horizons." Jacob beams.

Elliot's tongue darts from side to side, agitating one corner of his mouth, then the other, back and forth, back and forth. An expression of anthropological interest overhangs Michael's face. I am dumbfounded. Loss, failure, jealousy jumble in my head.

The phone rings into gaping silence.

"Mom, you're not answering my emails. Is he gone?"

"Oh Sarah, so much is happening."

Around the table the group leans in.

"Hang on, dear. I'll pick this up in the bedroom."

When I emerge a good twenty minutes later, Michael is bent over his cellphone, bag open at his feet.

He snaps the phone shut. Jacob and Elliott have gone to find a hotel room, he explains, for the short term at least. They'll be back at five. His voice thickens. "Perhaps we can meet here for a drink at the end of the afternoon, Michael. You must try one of his Bloody Marys, son. A taste sensation."

The imitation convulses me.

"The guy's a manipulator."

I nod.

Michael grasps my arm. "Listen, rehearsal's at noon and before that I need to see the allergist. But about last night, I mean, Lucy, you need to think seriously..."

"I know. It's time." I wipe my glasses on the hem of Sarah's shirt.

* * *

The Perlows are back at five on the dot, Elliott showered and shaved. His defining core of awkwardness remains. When Michael offers to mix some Bloody Marys, his face lifts.

"Thank you no, Michael," Jacob cuts in. His voice carries a new resolve. "Elliott and I must be totally clear-headed this evening. Of course, if you and Lucy..."

"Please," I break in. "Make yourselves comfortable."

He pauses until I am seated, then lowers himself toward the couch. Tinkers with his hearing aid. "I have come to a decision that may surprise you," he begins. A miniscule tremor has taken root in his left hand. "Reality forces me to the conclusion that a time will come when I may require skilled care and perhaps medical intervention. No, Lucy," he reads my face, "it is not helpful to avoid the truth. Mendel's option is extremely appealing." He works his mouth toward a half-smile. "As is Jose's. But the truth is, Riverdale Park can best provide those services."

A radiator pipe clangs in the bedroom.

"What proved intolerable at the Home, the total absence of privacy, is remediable, it turns out. Since my escape."

Elliott's face twitches upward.

"I have been on the telephone with the Home. Needless to say, they were thrilled to hear from me."

A giggle rises to my throat.

"At any rate, I presented to them a proposal which, after several backs and forths, has now been accepted. At my request, a written agreement is being drawn."

The clanging has escalated to bangs and hisses.

"In return for my total confidentiality in the matter of my escape, and also yours," Jacob levels a stern eye at each of us, "a private room will be made available, with a small refrigerator, so that I can entertain my friends, mix the occasional Bloody Mary if I choose. Yet to be worked out are some minor details." He smiles. "Small points when compared to the hint of a word dropped to a local tabloid." Beatifically the smile spreads outward over his face.

* * *

Several days have passed. Michael is practically moved in. We spend the evenings clearing drawers, consolidating closets, packing out-of-season clothing up onto unreachable shelves. The treadmill is even bulkier than I remembered.

Jacob and Elliott have been making short forays from their hotel into the neighborhood. When I stopped by their room yesterday on the way home from work, Jacob was already under the covers, gray with exhaustion. "It is time for me to settle into a simpler routine," he murmured.

The seventh morning. Michael wheels about the kitchen, whisking, folding, scrambling. I putter after him, light-headed, the way I felt when Sarah left for sleep-away camp the first time.

The social worker is here, her hair gathered into a no-nonsense ponytail. She's one of those seriously pleasant people who hold your gaze for a fraction of a second too long each time. We are gathered for a send-off brunch after which she will drive Jacob and Elliott up to the Home. Jacob's tremor is more pronounced this morning.

A group has gathered as we emerge from the elevator. I recognize Mendel and the newsstand owner.

"Yo Jacob," someone yells.

Jacob waves as he inches to the curb. As the social worker's car nears the corner, my face starts to crumble and Michael turns me back toward the elevator.

Later in the day I dial Jacob's new number at the Home. He was sleeping, I can tell. "No, no," he lies, covering the mouthpiece to hide a spasm of coughs. "Elliott just this moment left for the airport. I was considering perhaps catching a cat nap."

We drive up the next day after rehearsal, carting a monster sponge cake from Mendel. Dots of sunlight dance on the river, a few yellow leaves catch my eye.

My father is in the common room, gazing mildly in the direction of Regis on the tube. He looks frail, transparent.

"Poppa, come. We'll go into your bedroom where it's quiet."

On his sparse bed I massage cold cream onto the backs of his hands, the palms, the soft hollows between each finger. His skin gets so dry this time of year. Then Michael maneuvers the bulky wheelchair around the unit while I hang back, bantering with the other residents. Which of these mild, palsied old men is the sex-crazed roommate, I wonder?

Afterwards we visit with Jacob in his new digs, a corner room three floors down. Outside the window the river winds on and on. The cherry trees will be glorious in the spring.

Jacob has acquired a cane, a jazzy three-pronged number which he hands back and forth like Fred Astaire. It is impossible to check on the tremor. How is my father doing? He will stop by tomorrow and say hello to him. To everyone on the Unit. His face darkens. "Well, maybe not everyone." A Spanish language tape drones in the background, "*lunes, martes, miercoles...*"

ABOUT THE AUTHOR

 JUDITH FELSENFELD's early years were spent at the piano. She performed as a soloist and chamber pianist, and later moved on into performing arts management and development. Commuting back and forth between New York and Fort Lauderdale in the early '90s to care for her ailing mother, she began writing short stories. Her work has appeared in numerous publications, including the *Chicago Review* and the *Southwest Review*. Her story, "The Lover," was broadcast nationwide on NPR's Selected Shorts series of readings.

Judith and her husband, Carl, divide their time between New York City and the Hudson Valley, where she continues to write and plays chamber music.

CPSIA information can be obtained at www.ICGtesting.com
Printed in the USA
BVOW07s0715260614

357288BV00001B/8/P